AGNeS PARKeR...
HAPPY CAMPeR?

AGNeS PARKeR...
HAPPY CAMPeR?

by Kathleen O'Dell

Dial Books
New  York

DIAL BOOKS • A member of Penguin Group (USA) Inc. • Published by
The Penguin Group • Penguin Group (USA) Inc., 375 Hudson Street,
New York, NY 10014, U.S.A. • Penguin Group (Canada), 10 Alcorn
Avenue, Toronto, Ontario, Canada M4V 3B2 (a division of Pearson
Penguin Canada Inc.) • Penguin Books Ltd, 80 Strand, London WC2R
0RL, England • Penguin Ireland, 25 St. Stephen's Green, Dublin 2,
Ireland (a division of Penguin Books Ltd) • Penguin Group (Australia),
250 Camberwell Road, Camberwell, Victoria 3124, Australia (a division
of Pearson Australia Group Pty Ltd) • Penguin Books India Pvt Ltd, 11
Community Centre, Panchsheel Park, New Delhi-110 017, India •
Penguin Group (NZ), Cnr Airborne and Rosedale Roads, Albany,
Auckland 1310, New Zealand (a division of Pearson New Zealand Ltd) •
Penguin Books (South Africa) (Pty) Ltd, 24 Sturdee Avenue, Rosebank,
Johannesburg 2196, South Africa • Penguin Books Ltd, Registered
Offices: 80 Strand, London WC2R 0RL, England

Designed by Teresa Kietlinski
Text set in Berkeley Book
Printed in the U.S.A. on acid-free paper

10 9 8 7 6 5 4 3 2 1

Library of Congress Cataloging-in-Publication Data
O'Dell, Kathleen, date.
Agnes Parker . . . happy camper? / by Kathleen O'Dell ; illustrations by
Charise Mericle Harper.
    p. cm.
Sequel to: Agnes Parker . . . girl in progress.
Summary: Science camp brings pranks, fun, rivalries, and new insights
about a longtime best friend.
ISBN 0-8037-2962-6
[1. Camps—Fiction. 2. Best friends—Fiction. 3. Friendship—Fiction.]
I. Harper, Charise Mericle, ill. II. Title.
PZ7.O2325Ag 2005
[Fic]—dc22   2004008101

With love for my grandmother
Mary Heriza, Story Lady

AGNeS PARKeR...
HAPPY CAMPeR?

CHAPTER ONE

FOR THEIR FIRST DAY OF summer science camp, Agnes Parker and her best friend, Prejean Duval, are wearing dorky T-shirts that they bought last summer. Agnes's shows a wide-mouth bass with a thermometer in its mouth and the words FISH FEVER—CATCH IT! Prejean's is even uglier. It shows an angry trout in a suit and tie sitting at an office desk and reads: BORN TO FISH, FORCED TO WORK!

The T-shirts are man-sized and Agnes feels lost inside its nightgownish proportions. But Prejean, who has grown almost five inches since Christmas, somehow looks impossibly beautiful in hers.

"Oh, my goodness," Agnes hears Mrs. Parker say to Prejean's mother as they wait for the Camp Numanu bus. "Prejean is such a . . . swan!"

Mrs. Duval smiles and whispers, "Yes, but we don't talk about it. I don't want her to think it's some kind of accomplishment."

Agnes looks at Prejean bent over her duffel bag and wonders if she hears any of this. She gazes at the curve of Prejean's long neck. *Swan.* And then she touches her own. Wasn't it just last summer that she and her best friend wore the same-size everything? Aside from dorky T-shirts, she and Prejean don't exactly match anymore.

"So, I guess you guys like fishing?"

Agnes glances over her shoulder and sees Natalie Kim from their sixth-grade class. She feels grateful that Natalie is still very short. "Prejean's dad got these at a bait shop," says Agnes. "She begged him to let us have them."

"And they're so *you,*" says Natalie. "I mean, so *both of you.*"

"Speaking of 'both of you,'" says Prejean, yanking at her stuck duffel bag zipper, "where's Ashley?"

"At home," says Natalie.

"How come?" Agnes asks. She can't remember ever seeing Natalie Kim without Ashley Cardell.

"Well," says Natalie, "I asked her and she said, 'Like, why would I go away for four weeks of boring, icky science camp?'" She shrugs. "I'm just glad you guys are here. I don't see anyone else from our class."

"Nope," says Agnes. Then she tries to smile encouragingly. "But maybe someone will show up."

"Of course, you guys already requested the same cabin, right?" says Natalie.

"Of course!" says Prejean.

"Anyway," says Natalie, hugging herself, "maybe I'll get lucky and get in with you two."

"You know," says Prejean, nudging Agnes, "*I* almost ended up coming to camp alone too."

"Really?" says Natalie. "Didn't you want to go, Agnes?"

"Oh, I wanted to . . ." Agnes says.

"But she turned in the form a day late!" interrupts Prejean.

"Hey, my *mom* forgot about it," says Agnes. "I'm just lucky they took my application."

"True," says Prejean. "Because if you sent me off by myself, Agnes Parker, I would've had to kill you." Then she says to Natalie, "I'd still be here, though. My mom would have made me go."

Silent, Agnes shifts from one foot to the other. She'd never say so in front of newly orphaned Natalie, let alone Prejean, but Agnes wouldn't even dream of going to camp without her best friend.

"My mom leaves nothing to chance," says Natalie.

"She got my application in on the morning of the first day!"

"Yours too?" says Prejean, still trying to yank open her bag. "Oh, well. Maybe you'll get in with one of the eighth graders." Prejean looks up from her duffel and points at a snub-nosed girl playing cards, her mouth clamped down on a bubble gum cigar. "Remember Rita Morris? She used to go to our school."

Natalie frowns. "Yeah. Wasn't she always making those real loud burps? You know, in the halls?" She shakes her head. "I don't think she'd remember me."

Agnes can't help but picture herself, frozen with shyness, sitting next to Rita "The Burper" Morris on the bus. "Don't worry, Nat," she says. "You can hang out with us. Even if you're not in our cabin."

"Ah, I give up!" says Prejean. She dumps her duffel bag on the ground with a groan and starts wrestling with the ponytail clip holding back her mass of dark curls. As Prejean struggles with her magnificent cloud of hair, Agnes realizes that both she and Natalie are staring.

Prejean makes a face. "What are you guys looking at?" she says, instinctively wiping at her own nose.

"Uh, nothing," Agnes says.

"Well, I gotta see if my mom can unstick this stupid zipper." Prejean hoists the bag over her shoulder. "I'll be right back."

"Ohmigod," Natalie whispers to Agnes. "What happened to Prejean?"

"She grew," Agnes says.

"I'll say," Natalie says. "She's even taller than she was in June." She giggles. "You know," she says, lowering her voice, "when I first saw you guys across the parking lot, I thought, Wow. Who's that with Agnes? I mean, we're a little too old for babysitters, right?"

Agnes feels her smile go flat. Ugh. She's glad Prejean wasn't around to hear that.

A group of girls whoop as the yellow camp bus swings into the parking lot, and Agnes finally feels the jitters she's been fighting off all morning. "I gotta go see my mom," she says.

"That's my dad over there," says Natalie. "Four whole weeks. I can't tell you how many times my parents keep telling me I'm going to have *such a worthwhile experience!*"

As Agnes looks around for her own mother, she feels two hands on her shoulders.

"Well, I guess this is it," says Mrs. Parker.

Agnes turns and nods, resolutely avoiding the magnetic urge to throw her arms around her mother.

"So when you come home, you better know how to calculate the flow rate of a stream, etcetera. Because I'm going to be giving a very demanding test." Mrs. Parker smiles a little wistfully and Agnes can't resist.

She gives her mother a hard hug and leans into her shoulder.

"Thanks for hugging your old mother," says Mrs. Parker. "Have fun, honey."

"I will, I will!" says Agnes.

She watches as Prejean hugs her mom quickly, then backs away slowly, dragging her duffel as her mother gives her a list of last-minute instructions.

"And don't you lose anything!" says Mrs. Duval in her regal Jamaican accent. "All the underwear in that suitcase is *brand*-new!"

"Yes, Moth-er," says Prejean, waving good-bye. She shoots a look at Agnes that says, *C'mon, let's go!*

Just then the crowd of girls lined up for the bus start to sing what must be some campfire chant:

> *Take me there, I wanna go there.*
> *Take me there! I've been nowhere!*
> *Take me to that great place of wonders and wishes . . .*

"Well," says Prejean, "now we know who all the old eighth graders are."

"Does that mean we get to call ourselves seventh graders now?" Agnes asks.

"May as well," says Prejean. "It's a middle-school camp. Just think. Next summer, we'll be the ones who know all the stupid songs."

Agnes can't think that far ahead. All she knows is that the bus is chugging, the girls are shouting, and the fun she's looked forward to all summer is now just hours away. She glances over her shoulder and sees Natalie back toward the end of the line.

"I kind of feel sorry for Nat, being all alone."

"Me too," says Prejean. She shades her eyes with one hand and waves with the other. "Natalie!" she cries. "Over here!"

Agnes recognizes the grateful look on Natalie's face as she scurries to join them near the front of the line. The problem is, the girl in back of them won't budge, leaving Natalie and her luggage in a bump outside the line.

"'Scuse us," says Prejean. "Can you back up just a little bit?"

"So you can give cuts?" says the girl from behind.

"But she's with us," says Prejean.

"I know," says the girl. "And that's still cuts."

The girl has gray pointy glasses and wears unsummer-y oxfords. Her hair is chopped off in a way to suggest she snips it herself. With an axe.

"Okay," says Prejean. "It's cuts. Is that such a big deal to you?"

Natalie gives Agnes an *Uh-oh* look.

"What she means is," says Agnes, "do you mind? Because she's our friend. As a favor?"

The girl lifts one corner of her mouth. "Sure," says the girl calmly, "but only for you."

"Oh," says Agnes. "Well. Thanks."

"Because I prefer doing things for people who don't usually get their way," continues the girl. "And you strike me as that kind of person."

Agnes thinks this might be an insult, but there's nothing actually snotty in the girl's tone. "Well, like I said, thanks anyway. For the cuts," she stammers.

Prejean immediately pokes Agnes in the arm. "*Thank you?*" she says. "Oh, Agnes. That's, like, terminal ND."

"What's ND?" asks Natalie.

"Um," says Agnes, "it's a Prejean thing for . . . *niceness disease.*"

Natalie laughs. And Agnes laughs too. Sort of.

CHAPTER TWO

ON THE ROAD, AGNES WATCHES as the houses get more old-fashioned and far apart until finally there's nothing but cows and farmland. Natalie is sitting in the seat before them. She and Prejean talk up a storm.

"Did you know," says Prejean, "that my mom bought three different sizes of permanent marker. Three! She put my name on everything. Even my toothbrush."

"My mother," says Natalie, "printed out a million and one NATALIE KIM sticky labels. Everything else has official NATALIE KIM cloth labels sewn in by hand!"

"Ha!" Prejean continues. "Mine actually had to wear

these magnifying glasses to write my name in teeny letters. I'm surprised she didn't write all over *me* . . ."

Agnes wrote all her labels on her stuff herself with a purple pen from her art supply box.

"Whoo-hoo! Look!" says Prejean.

The sign for Camp Numanu points down a rutted, woodsy road. Jouncing, Agnes feels her heart beat faster. When they pull up to cabins clustered around the main lodge, there are several parked school buses and a crowd of girls milling.

"This is it," says Natalie, surveying the crowd of potential bunkmates.

"Yep," says Agnes, trying to be encouraging. "And it's going to be fun, right?"

The doors of the bus swing open and the campers pile out. When Agnes looks around, she's nose to nose with that girl with the chopped hair and pointy glasses.

"Hey," Agnes says, feeling awkward. She looks down at the curled-up magazine in the girl's hand. Something called . . . *DREAD*? "We're here," she says.

"Yes." The girl's mouth is a straight line and her gray eyes a neutral blank. "We are."

Agnes, stumped for conversation, turns around. *Geez,* she thinks, and quickly decides to keep her distance.

Once outside, she sees that the cabins are all alike except for the wooden plaques over the door. Each one is named after a forest creature. BEAR, WOOD DOVE, RACCOON . . .

An athletic-looking woman with short gray hair and military posture holds up her hand and blasts her whistle. "Okay, campers. Listen up! I'm Mrs. Finney . . ."

"FIN-NEY!" a group of eighth graders chant like a bunch of rowdy football players.

Tweeeeeeeep! goes the whistle. Finney makes a *Cut it* motion across her neck, and everyone quiets. "That's better!" she continues. "I'm Camp Numanu's director and I'm looking forward to meeting each and every one of you. In fact, everyone here has been looking forward to the arrival of this bus! Because now we can get down to the business of assigning your cabins.

"RED SQUIRRELS!" says Mrs. Finney. "Lana Meyers and Shawn Levitz!"

Meyers and Levitz walk up to Mrs. Finney with their arms around each other's shoulders as the girls clap and scream.

"Ann Carstairs and Trini Kajanian!" More shrieks.

Two by two the girls are called until Red Squirrel has their eight campers.

"Whew," says Natalie. "I'm sort of glad I didn't make Squirrels."

"I know," agrees Agnes. "Too obnoxious."

"Next, FAWNS!" announces Mrs. Finney.

"Nadia Volk and Lisa Runelson! Sandra Chambers and Isabella Falk."

Agnes keeps one eye on Natalie as she clenches and unclenches her fists.

"Dara Dearborn and Hailey Sibert! Prejean Duval and . . ." Here, Mrs. Finney squints at the clipboard. Prejean gives Agnes a goofy, expectant smile.

"Natalie Kim!" cries Mrs. Finney.

"Huh?" says Agnes. All three girls stare at each other open-mouthed. Mrs. Finney looks around over the heads of the crowd.

"Duval?" she says. "Kim?"

"Don't worry," Prejean says to Agnes. She jogs up to Mrs. Finney and starts gesturing, pointing at Agnes and talking a mile a minute.

Agnes's heart sinks as she sees Mrs. Finney shake her head.

Oh . . . c'mon! thinks Agnes.

"Girls! Look here!" Mrs. Finney opens her hands like a book and pretends to read. "As stated on the application, there is no guarantee about requesting bunkmates. Now," she says, closing her "book," "it's important to just keep this process moving."

Natalie glances over at Agnes. "I'm really sorry," she says quietly, and then runs off to join Prejean.

"WOOD DOVES!" says Mrs. Finney. Agnes stands stunned as the Fawns circle together with their cabin counselors. Prejean looks over her shoulder at Agnes and then glances up to the sky as if to say, *Why?*

But Agnes knows why. The stupid application. Who knows how long it took to get from the mailbox to the actual camp? *Late, late, late.* For the first time in her life, Agnes wishes her mother was more like Mrs. Duval.

As the cabins are called, Agnes crosses her fingers. It's that same feeling she gets when they're picking teams for gym, only worse. She tries to appear cool, but mentally she is dog-paddling furiously. *What if I'm not even registered at all?*

"Final cabin!" says Mrs. Finney. "MALLARD!"

Agnes counts the remaining girls. Including herself, there are only seven.

"Agnes Parker and Nyssa Vanderhoven!"

Nothing.

Agnes raises her hand, identifying herself to her new bunkmate. And then the chopped-off-hair girl rises from the ground where she has been out of sight, absorbed in her magazine.

Agnes's hand drops. *Of all the possible Nyssa Vanderhovens.* Agnes tries not to look as disappointed as she feels. "It's . . . you," she says.

"Yes," Nyssa says. "It is me. So, Agnes Parker, are fish murder T-shirts big where you come from?"

"No, I mean . . . not really. What?" says Agnes.

Nyssa reopens her magazine. "I'm a conscientious

21

objector," she says with a deeply focused weariness. "I won't kill fish."

"Oh, I don't think they force anyone to kill fish at this camp," Agnes says. "But some of the girls are going to try fly-fishing."

"I also refuse to *witness* people killing fish," says Nyssa, turning a page.

Up ahead, the two Mallard camp counselors are waiting for Agnes and Nyssa with outstretched arms. One teenager is tall and skinny, with a camouflage hat pulled down over her eyes. The other is short, stocky, and frizzy-haired, wearing a straw hat with pom-pom fringe. Both counselors throw their hands in the air. "We have baby MALLARDS!" they cry.

Agnes and Nyssa stand stiffly as both girls rush toward them for a crushing hug.

"And look," says the short counselor. "They both come with glasses!"

Agnes feels herself blushing so badly that she wants to put her hands over her face.

"Oops, I can tell these two aren't huggers," says the tall girl in a confidential drawl.

"That's cool, because this is just a one-time welcome hug. Then we promise to stop." The short girl smiles. "I'm Tiki," she says. "And this is your cocounselor, Willow."

"I'm Agnes."

"HI, AGNES!" says a voice from behind. It's a black-haired girl in ripped jeans, waving her fishing pole.

"We were Mallards last year too," says her friend, the most freckled kid Agnes has ever seen.

"This," says the fishing-pole girl, pointing to her friend, "is SPF."

"My real name is Sara Patrice Freilicher," says SPF.

"And she has to wear, like, 100 SPF sunscreen," says the girl with the fishing pole. "Or she fries."

"And that's George Alvarez," says SPF. "The first name's short for Georgina."

"I hate my name," volunteers George. "Anyone who calls me Georgina will wake up with shaving cream on their pillow." Then she turns to Nyssa. "And you, newcomer Mallard. What is your name?"

Nyssa stands with her hands by her sides. She looks at the fishing pole and then to Georgina's face. "I'm Nyssa," she says flatly. "Just Nyssa. I don't do nicknames."

George's mouth makes an *O*. "Did I say something?" she whispers to SPF.

Agnes wants to get off to a friendlier start and almost butts in and tells them some explanation about Nyssa's strong attachment to fish. But then she decides against it.

"Didn't they just announce Lisette and Beth?" says Tiki, glancing over her shoulders.

"Here!" says a mousy girl, poking her wispy-haired head from behind a tree.

"Me too," says the other girl in an identical whispery voice.

Agnes can't believe her eyes when the two girls get closer. She has seen identical twins before, but these are the most identical ever.

"I'm Beth," says the one on the right.

"I'm Lisette," says the one on the left.

Agnes makes a mental note: *Red shorts, Lisette.*

"We have two more Mallards coming," says Willow. "But Finney says they're in the john. They'll catch up with us at the cabin."

"Okay, girls!" says Willow. "Are you ready for the best summer of your life? With the best buddies you'll ever have? In the best cabin Camp Numanu has EVER SEEN?"

"MAL-LARDS!" cheers Tiki. "Say it with me!"

"Mallards!" The girls sort of cheer.

"You can do better than that!" says Willow.

"Mallards!" they say again.

"Nuh-uh," says Tiki. "I want to hear you loud and clear. Each and every one. Now . . . MAL-LARDS!"

Agnes sucks in her breath and roars 'til her throat hurts. All the girls do.

Except for Nyssa, who makes a point of saying "ducks" in her matter-of-fact way.

CHAPTER THREE

ON THE TRAIL TO THE Mallard cabin, Nyssa imparts some important information to Agnes.

"One," she says, ticking a finger, "you are my so-called bunk buddy. Which means you and me—we're stuck together."

"Uh-huh," says Agnes, craning her neck, hoping for a glimpse of Prejean.

"Two," says Nyssa, "if you are all into being a happy camper, I am going to disappoint you. A lot."

"I'm not disappointed," Agnes says bravely.

"Because, three, I was really hoping that I wouldn't get a bunk buddy. And that's not personal to you,

Agnes Parker. But I am completely honest. Always."

"Well, I'm honest too," Agnes says, squaring her shoulders.

"No, you think you're honest. But what you really are is nice. Whereas I am extremely, *extremely* honest." Nyssa gives Agnes a penetrating stare. "You will probably end up hating me."

Agnes considers this. "What if I refuse to hate you?" she asks.

"Then that will just prove that you're not really acting honestly. Which brings me back to what I said before about you only thinking you are honest."

But what Agnes is really thinking is: *Help!*

The Mallard cabin sits at the outer edge of the campground. "Home sweet home!" Tiki announces. Willow steps up to the cabin's stoop and opens the door.

"Wait up!" Agnes sees big eighth grader Rita Morris dragging an extraordinarily tiny camper by the hand. "Sorry," says Rita. "Kacy here had to go to the 'little girls' room.' Get it?"

"My hand is turning purple," Kacy says in a high, helium voice.

Rita doesn't let go. Agnes wonders if the towering Rita can hear Kacy all the way down there.

"I was a Red Squirrel last year," Rita says. "And Kacy will be a new seventh grader at my school."

Rita yanks Kacy's arm in the air. "Lookit how little she is."

"I skipped two grades," says Kacy.

Is that all? Agnes wonders. This girl could pass for a fourth grader, easy.

"Bet she's smart, huh?" says Rita.

"Can I have my arm back," Kacy asks, jiggling her knees. "Please?"

Rita drops the hand and pats Kacy gently on top of the head. "Sorry," she says.

"Come in!" says Willow. "Y'all are just in time for the sacred initiation!"

Inside, there are five bunks neatly made up with gray wool blankets.

"Stow your stuff beneath the beds and join us in a circle, please!" Tiki cries.

"Which bed?" Agnes asks Nyssa.

"Doesn't matter."

Agnes throws her duffel beneath the nearest bunk.

"*But,*" says Nyssa, "if you're a wiggly sleeper, you have to take the bottom bunk. I need the bed to be *very still.*"

"I'm not sure what kind of sleeper I am," says Agnes.

"Then you're down here. And I'm on top," Nyssa states.

"Now you must sit with us," says Willow, "as we serenade you."

Agnes joins the circle of Mallards, squeezing in

between Willow and Tiki. Each takes one of her hands as they begin to sing.

You're one of us. We'll watch your back!
O'er forest trails with canvas pack!
Through sunrise, moon, and dawn's first crack,
If you need us, give a Mal-lard QUACK!

"That quack," says Willow, in her slowed-down cowboy drawl, "is our call of friendship to each other. We don't yell, applaud, or wave. We quack. If you need help from a buddy, quack. So, can I hear y'all?"

"*Quack . . . quack . . . quack . . .*"

Agnes notices that everyone at least tries to sound like a real, live duck.

Tiki and Willow make the Mallards sing the anthem several times until everyone has it memorized.

"Good! And although *all* Mallards are friends to the end," says Tiki, "you especially don't let your bunk-mate down! You sleep together, work together . . ."

"You're a team," says Willow. "And now, as part of our team-buildin' rite of passage, it's your turn to sing to your bunkmate." She holds Agnes's hand in the air. "How about it, Agnes?"

"Really?" says Agnes. She looks across the circle at Nyssa, who is studying her thumb tips.

"It's not hard," says Willow. "Just repeat every line

after Nyssa says it. Then you'll be her official bunk buddy."

"And an official Mallard!" proclaims Tiki.

At once, the Mallards give a chorus of quacks. All of them seem directed at Nyssa, who stares back like a suspect in a police lineup.

Finally, someone barks, "Get over here, Nyssa!" It's Rita. She's puffing out her cheeks with impatience.

"We're supposed to *quack*, Rita," says Kacy in her munchkin squeak.

"I've already quacked," says Rita. "Now she's supposed to come over."

Agnes wraps her arms around herself tight.

"Now, now," says Tiki.

Agnes watches as Tiki fetches Nyssa. She practically has to drag her over.

"I don't think," says Agnes, "that Nyssa should have to sing if she doesn't want to. I mean, it's okay with me."

Rita raises her hand. "No fair!" she says to Tiki.

"Agnes," says Willow gently, "we all follow the same rules here."

"And the same traditions!" Tiki adds brightly.

"It's a big part of what Camp Numanu is all about," continues Willow. "And you know that, don't you, Nyssa?"

"Yes," Nyssa says.

"That's better!" Tiki smiles.

"I don't want to do it," says Nyssa frankly, "but it's a rule. And by staying here, I've agreed to obey the rules."

"Well, okay!" says Tiki.

Nyssa drops her eyes to half mast. She opens her mouth and sings in a monotone:

"We're one of two. I'll watch your back."

Agnes looks at Tiki and Willow, who both nod encouragingly. Nyssa has started out in a key so low, Agnes has to growl to reach it.

"We're one of two. I'll watch your back." There are some giggles. I sound like a bear, thinks Agnes.

"O'er forest trails with canvas pack." Nyssa continues, in an even lower voice.

Agnes coughs. *"O'er forest trails with canvas pack."*

"Through sunrise, moon, and dawn's first crack . . ." sings Nyssa, even lower.

Agnes chokes out the phrase.

"If you need me—just give a QUACK!" concludes Nyssa. Her quack sounds like a belch.

Agnes simply cannot go any lower. She takes a breath and switches keys. *"If you need me, just give a quack!"*

Ack! Now she is squeaking like an opera lady. The Mallards laugh.

Nyssa lifts one corner of her mouth in a sort of smile. Agnes grits her teeth. Butt-head! she thinks.

"Wonderful!" says Tiki. "You are now joined in bunk-buddyhood, 'til the end of camp do you part!"

"Whoo-hoo!" the Mallards cheer. Agnes sees red-faced Rita scowling and tiny Kacy with her hands tucked protectively under her armpits. George whispers vigorously into SPF's ear. Lisette and Beth sit unblinking as two matching dolls. Eager Tiki grins while slouchy Willow pulls her hat down even farther over her eyes.

Agnes lets it sink in. These are my people, she thinks. My four-week people.

After all the Mallards finish their bunkmate serenades, it's time for lunch. Agnes can hardly wait to get outside and spill the whole story about her incredible roommate to Prejean. She walks swiftly, scanning all the outdoor picnic tables.

"Yoo-hoo! Agnes! My dah-ling!" Prejean is sitting at a far table, waving her arms. The sight of her smiling friend fills Agnes with relief.

"Coming, my sweet!" Agnes waves back.

"My sweet?" says Nyssa, grimacing.

"Uh, yes. That's just some jokey junk we say," says Agnes nervously. "Anyway, I gotta go see her."

"Go," sighs Nyssa. "But you'll be back."

In her flying haste, Agnes catches her toe on a tree root and almost falls on her face.

"Careful," cries Prejean, catching her by the arm.

Agnes notices that Prejean is wearing a bead and

leather bracelet. Natalie is wearing one too. "Did you guys make these?" Agnes asks.

"Yep," says Natalie. "I made that one for Prejean, and she made this one for me." Natalie holds out her arm for Agnes's inspection.

"Oh," says Agnes. "Nice!"

"What cabin you in?" Natalie asks.

"Mallard," says Agnes.

"What's your bunk buddy like?" says Prejean, flashing a pained squint.

When Agnes sees that Natalie is making the exact same sympathy face, she's suddenly bugged. "She's, uh, I don't know," says Agnes.

"Is she at least nice?" Prejean asks.

"Actually, you know her. She's that girl from the bus. Who wouldn't give you cuts?"

"You're kidding," says Prejean. "Yuck!"

"Poor Agnes," says Natalie to Prejean.

Something about the way Natalie says this, the way she turns to Prejean as if they're having a *private understanding,* really annoys Agnes. "Oh, she's not that bad," she finds herself insisting. "I actually kind of like her. And anyway, who says I can't hang out with you guys at lunch and stuff?"

Natalie gives Agnes an even sadder look, and Prejean says quickly, "Agnes, you can't eat with the Fawns."

"Why?" Agnes asks.

"Because you have to eat with your cabin. We do camp things even at meals. There are meetings and competitions and stuff." Prejean shrugs. "I know. It's dumb."

Agnes slumps. "Oh."

"Your counselors didn't tell you this stuff?" Natalie asks.

"I kind of didn't give them the chance," Agnes says. Suddenly she hears, "Quack! Calling Agnes Parker! *Quaaack!*" She looks over and sees Willow waving her arms.

"I guess that's for you?" says Prejean. "Now, don't worry. You'll see us around."

"I'm *not* worried," Agnes says emphatically. She walks back to the Mallards feeling much more irritated than she did even five minutes ago.

Agnes eyes the Mallard table and sees Nyssa hasn't saved a place for her. Tiki, though, leaps up immediately.

"Come right here and sit by me," she says. When she shakes her head, the pom-poms hanging from the brim of her straw hat do a little rumba.

When it's the Mallards' turn at the chuck wagon, George motions for Agnes to stand in line. "Look," she says, "if you need to talk to anybody, just come to me and SPF. You know what I mean?"

Agnes, still flustered, says, "I think so…"

"Really. Don't be shy," says SPF. "Me and George met here, but we were so lucky. It was like we knew each other in a past life."

"And we realize," continues George, "that any one of us could've gotten stuck with the Sour Patch Kid."

Agnes looks over her shoulder toward the back of the line. Can Nyssa hear what they're saying?

"Mm, thanks, guys," Agnes says. She grabs a sandwich and fruit and hurries back to the table. As she passes her bunk buddy, she tries to give her a friendly, reassuring look. It's just too early to write her, or any of us, off, she thinks.

When the girls are seated, Willow claps her hands above her head. "Cabin announcements!" she shouts. Three of the Mallards immediately break into another song:

> *Announce-ments, announce-ments!*
> *Close your mouth and open your ears!*
> *Announcements!*

"Thank you, Mallards," says Willow. "Tomorrow at campfire, we are having a special event. Now, I want you all to listen to this announcement with an OPEN MIND!"

Agnes hesitates to join in as some of the girls begin

quacking. George motions to Agnes, making a little duck puppet with her hand.

"Oh, quack quack," says Agnes.

"We are having a costume extravaganza!"

Agnes, feeling excited, gives a loud quack-quack, and quickly realizes that everyone else is silent.

"Thank you, Camper Agnes," Willow says. "Now for the rest of you—didn't I say keep an open mind? This is what you call a creative exercise and it does relate to science."

"It's not a fashion show," says Tiki. "Each cabin will represent one of our study units."

"Ours is aquatic life," says Willow. "We drew that from a hat."

Tiki nods. "And the boys' camp is doing it too," she says. "It should be really fun!"

"And funny!" says Willow. "Believe me, we did it last year and it was a blast!"

"That sounds fun!" squeaks Kacy. Rita nods approvingly.

"As long as I don't have to model," says George.

"Ditto!" says SPF.

Lisette whispers into Beth's ear. "We don't want to model either," she says in her airy voice.

"Please," Lisette whispers, crowding even closer to Beth.

Kacy pipes up. "I can't do it, because . . ." she

says, smiling proudly, "you guys are gonna need me to do hair."

Rita bends down. "You know how to do that all by yourself?"

Kacy draws herself up. "I am *not* a baby!" she cries.

"Or course you're not, little Bunky," Rita says, reaching over. But Kacy clamps her hands to her head before Rita can pat her.

"Now, I'd say yes," continues Rita, "only I did it last year and I think it should be someone else's turn."

"Nyssa?" asks Tiki. "Would you help us out?"

The girls quiet down to hear Nyssa's answer.

"I'll help," she says. "I have, you know, some ideas."

Tiki gives her a dazzling smile. "Fabulous!"

"BUT," says Nyssa, with a sly sidelong glance, "I think Agnes would make the *best* model. She already has on a fish shirt."

Agnes looks down at her chest. *Fish Fever!*

"You know, Nyssa," says Tiki, "I think you've got something there."

Agnes likes making costumes, but modeling them is another thing. As Tiki and Willow gaze at her imploringly, she can read the thought bubble over their heads. *PLEASE, PLEASE, CAMPER AGNES! BE OUR MALLARD MODEL!*

And then she hears herself say, "Okay."

"Let's hear it!" says Willow.

Quacks resound. And clapping. "Yay, Agnes!" say George and SPF.

"It'll be easy!" says Tiki, giving Agnes a pat on the back.

Easy as falling of a cliff, she wants to say. But instead, in her old Agnes way, she looks back at Tiki and smiles.

CHAPTER FOUR

AGNES WAKES UP THINKING VAGUELY that someone lowered the ceiling during the night. And then, after inhaling the scent of pine needles in the strangely chilly air, she realizes where she is. She lies on her back, sighs, and gazes at the mattress above.

Nyssa Vanderhoven . . .

From somewhere in the forest, a trumpet blows clumsily and off-key.

"Reveille!" shouts Tiki. Willow drops from the top bunk wearing a tank top and boxer shorts printed all over with dice. Agnes stares at her knobby knees as she stands at attention.

Tiki salutes. "Up and at 'em, Mallards!"

George stands and pokes SPF sharply with her forefinger. "C'mon, Bunky," she says.

"Bluh," says SPF. "This is the only part of camp that I hate."

Lisette and Beth slip noiselessly out of their bunks. Agnes notices that even though they're wearing full-length nightgowns, they're crossing their arms over their chests as if they were naked.

Agnes is about to sit up when Nyssa hangs over the edge of her bed, her hair hanging blunt as a whisk broom.

"Good morning," Agnes says.

"*You,*" says Nyssa, "are a wiggler."

Agnes opens her mouth as Nyssa's head disappears. *I slept like a brick!* she wants to say. But then she can't help feeling that someone's eyes are upon her. It's Rita Morris giving her the squint.

"Heyyy," says Rita. "*Now* I know who you are. It's been driving me crazy!"

"Yeah," says Agnes, rising. "You used to go to my school."

"But you must've gotten glasses, right?"

"Yep," says Agnes.

"You used to hang out with that other kid . . ."

"Prejean Duval," Agnes says.

"Right-o," she says, cocking her finger at Agnes like a little gun.

Tiki quacks everyone quiet. Agnes listens as Willow tells them the morning routine: twenty minutes for bed-making, dressing, and bathroom, then breakfast at the lodge.

Agnes hurries, thinking maybe she can get in a little talking time with Prejean. She's got everything done and is exiting the bathroom when she hears Willow say:

"Remember, this first week is for Mallards only. Okay? Sit with your bunk buddy and I want you each to come up with five questions to ask each other."

"Can't we even talk to any of the girls in the other cabins?" Agnes whispers to SPF.

"Huh-uh. Not for a week, Camper Agnes," Willow says.

"Sorry about that, my Mallard friend," says George.

When Nyssa joins the three girls, Agnes's eyes are drawn to her chest. In the middle of her T-shirt are the tiny letters: GRRRRR.

"You ready?" Agnes asks.

"As I'll ever be," says Nyssa.

Five questions. Agnes isn't so nervous about what she'll ask Nyssa as about what Nyssa might ask her. She tags along a step behind as Nyssa loads up on pancakes from the cafeteria line, then follows her to the Mallard table.

As the two sit down, sudden squeals erupt at a distant table. Agnes cranes her neck and sees—Prejean! She's being hugged like a Miss America contestant by a gang of those Fawns. And her hair is up on top in this weird ponytail that spouts like a fountain. All the Fawns have the same cheerleader hairstyle tied up with matching polka-dot ribbons. *What in the world . . . ?*

"Okay," says Nyssa. "Here's my first question: When you look at the Fawns and the Mallards, do you get the idea there's some kind of conspiracy?"

"I don't get what you mean," Agnes says.

"Well, look at them. All sort of beautifully girly and shrieky. And look at us: glasses, flat-chested, nerdy." Nyssa pauses. "It's like they assigned us to cabins in order of personal attractiveness."

Agnes straightens her glasses. "Rita Morris isn't flat-chested," protests Agnes.

"No," says Nyssa, "but you don't see any Fawns with a nose like Rita's."

"Uh, George is cute," says Agnes. "Sporty-cute."

"Yeah," says Nyssa. "But in an un-white, inner-city sort of way."

"Well, that's not fair. The Fawns have Prejean," says Agnes. "And she's . . . un-white."

"I dispute that," Nyssa states. "Completely. *I'm* blacker than Prejean."

Agnes feels herself turning hot. "What a crummy thing to say! How can you pretend to know anything about her?"

"Because it's obvious. I mean, she doesn't talk like any African American girls I know. In fact, she talks like YOU. And how black is that?" Nyssa asks.

"I don't see how—"

"AND," interrupts Nyssa, "she's just too entitled in that cheerleader-y, knows-she's-so-beautiful way."

Agnes can't believe how far off the mark Nyssa is. Prejean may be bossy, but "knows-she's-so-beautiful"? Prejean became beautiful only very recently, and Agnes is sure that she doesn't even know it yet! Agnes clenches her jaw. "My turn for a question. Nyssa Vanderhoven, where do you live?"

"In the un-white inner city," she says. "Now my turn. Why do you wiggle so much when you sleep?"

"Why does it bother you so much if I wiggle when I sleep?"

"Because I can't sleep with wiggling," returns Nyssa.

"What do you want me to do?" asks Agnes.

"Stop wiggling!" says Nyssa.

"How?" Agnes asks, her voice rising. "I'm asleep!"

"I don't know. Meditation?" suggests Nyssa.

Agnes splutters, "Oh Nyssa! Why are you so . . . *so* . . . THE WAY YOU ARE?"

"I could answer that," Nyssa says, her gray eyes glinting, "but you've already asked your five questions!"

Agnes trembles. She stands up. "I'm going to get seconds," she says, grabbing her completely full plate.

What a nasty, rotten, snotty, horrible girl, thinks Agnes as she stumbles off. How can anyone even think such things about Prejean—or me!

"Pssst! Agnes!"

Out of the corner of her eye, Agnes sees someone trying to catch up with her. Prejean!

"Look, come with me through the food line," Prejean says, "so then we can talk."

"Yes, yes!" says Agnes. "But first, you gotta tell me: What's with the hair?"

Prejean rolls her eyes. "It was this Dara girl's idea. She was a Fawn last year, so she brought this ribbon. Brown with spots. Fawn. Get it? Me and Natalie didn't want to do it, but…"

"I know," says Agnes quickly. "You just don't want to make a fuss."

"Exactly," says Prejean, setting some juice on her tray. "I tell you, I'm just so, so lucky to have Nat. She's a blast. I wish you could get to know her too."

Agnes pulls her mouth into a smile that feels absolutely fake. "Yeah? Well. I'm having a blast too," she says through her teeth.

Prejean raises an eyebrow. "Really?"

"Yeah!" Agnes says, wishing she didn't sound as annoyed as the question made her feel. "So, um, how come everyone over there is hugging you?"

"Because," Prejean says, "they voted me to be their

model." She sticks out her tongue. "For the camp-fire?"

"Oh! Wow," says Agnes. "Me too! But only because nobody else would do it."

Prejean stuffs a piece of paper into Agnes's hand. "We're gonna get in trouble if we keep blabbing."

"See you at campfire," says Agnes.

Prejean walks off, giving Agnes a brisk backward wave. Agnes, anxious to read the note, slips into a corner and unfolds it.

Agnes:

You know how much I hate writing. I must like you and miss you very much to sit down with a pen and scribble things.

The girls in our cabin I can only describe as <u>fluffy</u>. 3 different people came up to me in the first hour and asked me WHAT I was. Like I was a vegetable or a rock or something. So I kept on saying GIRL. Or HUMAN. Then they finally ask if I'm AFRICAN AMERICAN. I tell them no, my Dad is French/Canadian and Mom is from Jamaica. At least Natalie gets it. One girl keeps calling her "that Chinese girl." Nat told her NO! KOREAN! And a couple of girls said isn't that the same thing?

This morning when they said we were having pancakes Natalie says to me: I cannot cope without my chopsticks. And I said, what are these round cakes? Does no one understand my island ways? So many clueless people.

We need some normal girls. And I need my best friend.
I could go on.
LOVE, PREJEAN

So Prejean is dealing with weird people too? The letter makes Agnes feel less creeped out about Prejean's new funny hairdo, and other stuff too. Even, almost, the newfound friendship with Natalie part.

Agnes feels ready to face Nyssa now. When she returns to the table, she sits beside her and gives her a snarky *Who needs you?* "quack."

"Quack back," Nyssa says blandly.

Then Tiki motions for everyone to stand. "Time for work, Mallards!" she announces.

"What work?" Agnes asks.

"You missed it, Agnes," says George. "We're doing dirt today."

"As in studying soil," says SPF. "With this teacher guy who's actually named Sandy."

"Hmm," says Agnes. "Interesting."

"You bet it is," says Nyssa, suddenly passionate. "It's full of nutrients and microorganisms and it's totally a valuable part of the ecosystem."

Yikes, thinks Agnes. She's just so strange.

"Think *she's* weird?" whispers George. "Wait 'til you meet Sandy!"

Sandy turns out to be a grandfatherly man who

winks a lot. Agnes sees nothing strange at all about him until he picks up a palmful of dirt . . . and swallows it.

"*Ewwwww!*" go the girls.

"I did that to get your attention!" He smiles, dirt clinging around his mouth like dry brownie mix. "Because I know you girls. Most of you hate dirt, right?" he says, staring directly at the silently shocked identical twins.

"Are we supposed to like it?" ventures Beth. Or Lisette.

"NO!" Sandy shouts. "Of course not. Nobody's supposed to love dirt! Dirt is germy awful stuff—a form of garbage, you might say. But soil . . ." Here he smiles again, showing his muddy teeth. "Soil is nature's perfect food. We do not call it dirt. Get me?"

"It's SOIL," says Rita. She smiles. "We learned that last year in Red Squirrels."

"Good for you, miss," says Sandy. "Then you must also know that not all soil is the same. Nope. There's all different kinds. And that's what we're going to discover today!"

Sandy divides the Mallards into two groups and gives each a box-shaped metal gutter with one pointed end and a handle at the other. "What we're going to do is drive this thing into the ground. You can take turns whacking it. It's heavy work."

"We didn't do this last year," says Rita.

"Of course not!" says Sandy. "We gotta change the curriculum every other year for you returning campers."

"But what about my little bunk buddy?" Rita hoists Kacy under the arms and holds her up like a doll. "She's no bigger than a bump on a pickle."

Kacy's legs kick back and forth.

"Put her down, Morris!" snaps Nyssa.

"Down!" squeals Kacy.

"Little, I mean, younger people are persons too," says Nyssa.

Rita, catching Kacy's fierce expression, drops her immediately. "Geez. Sorry," Rita mumbles. "Didn't mean anything."

Kacy crosses her arms. "Hmph!" she says.

Nyssa and Agnes are paired off with George and SPF. Tiki stands by with a mallet. "Who goes first?" she asks brightly.

"Maybe me?" says SPF. "It's probably best to go from tallest to shortest."

"Good thinking, Mallard," says Tiki. "This gutter stands pretty high until it gets hammered down a bit." Tiki holds the metal with the sharp stake side on top of the soil. "George? You come here and hold it steady."

"Don't worry, Georgie," says SPF. "I'll be really careful." She shakily hoists the mallet to shoulder level and tap-taps the gutter until it's buried about a foot in the ground.

"Whew!" says Tiki. "Great job! Next?"

"That's me!" volunteers George. Agnes notices that even though George is shorter, she handles the mallet without a wobble. Ka-chunk! With one blow the gutter settles in another foot.

"Now you," says Nyssa to Agnes.

Don't boss me around, thinks Agnes, sure that she and Nyssa are about the same size. "Oh, fine, whatever!" she says, reaching for the mallet. When George hands it over, Agnes finds she has underestimated the weight of the thing. She doesn't grasp the handle down far enough and the oversized hammer drops from her grip. She leaps aside.

"Augh!" cries Nyssa. "Gawd!" She hops around holding her left foot. Her face is screwed up in pain.

"Oh!" says Agnes, horrified. "I'm so, *so* sorry! You okay?"

"It's . . . my little toe," gasps Nyssa, wincing.

"Nyssa, honey," says Tiki, "as soon as you stop jumping, we gotta take a look at that foot."

"I'm sorry, Nyssa," says Agnes, hands balled up under her chin. "Should we call someone? This is so awful."

"Excuse me, Agnes," says Tiki. "I've got to get Nyssa's shoe off." She takes the mallet from the ground and hands it, very carefully, to Agnes.

Agnes holds on to the hammer for dear life. "George? Will you take this out of my hands, please? I don't want a turn."

"Sure," says George, grabbing the mallet as if it were a pencil.

As George resumes hammering the gutter into the ground, Agnes peeks over at Nyssa's bare foot. Her little toe is already dark purple.

"Can you wiggle it?" asks Tiki.

Nyssa screws up her face. "Uh-huh. It still moves."

"Well, it's probably not broken then. You're lucky you were wearing those big shoes."

Agnes feels a terrible heaviness welling up beneath her ribs. Guilt. When she finally meets eyes with Nyssa, the feeling doubles. She knows what Nyssa's thinking—that Agnes did it on purpose. Or, rather, *accidentally on purpose.*

After all, if she'd had an opportunity to drop a hammer on her toe at breakfast, wouldn't she have wanted to?

No! Agnes shrugs off the thought. *Of course not.* She has never hit or hurt anyone in her entire life.

Until now?

Meanwhile, George and SPF are pulling the gutter out of the ground with some help from Sandy. They gasp at what they see. Ribbons of soil in different colors all the way down in spicy colors as varied and pretty as the walls of the Grand Canyon.

"What do you think?" Sandy asks, beaming.

"It's beautiful," Agnes says. Who would've thought?

She goes up to the gutter and runs her hand down the layers of soil. It's enough to give her a new reverence for dirt, uh, soil.

She turns to say something to Nyssa, only to see her limping, one arm around Tiki's neck, to Finney's office. Is this the last of Nyssa she'll ever see?

Chapter Five

When Agnes does see Nyssa next at lunch, she's wearing flip-flops and an oversized bandage on her injured toe. With a thump-clumping lurch, Nyssa picks up a tray and heads for the outdoor lunch cart.

Agnes takes a deep breath and runs over to meet her. "Let me take your tray for you," she says.

"I'm fine," Nyssa says.

"No, really. Let me. Please."

Nyssa stops in her tracks. "Agnes," she says firmly. "Listen!"

Agnes braces herself for a lecture.

"Agnes," repeats Nyssa, more evenly, "I don't blame you."

"You don't?"

"No. I don't."

The expression on Nyssa's face is a new one. Her gray eyes aren't steely. It's as if she's letting Agnes look in.

"Well, maybe you should blame me," says Agnes. "I've been doing a lot of thinking. Trying to be honest. You know—your area of expertise."

She sees Nyssa smile in her subtle, one-sided way.

"Because," continues Agnes, "I was totally mad at you. So . . . maybe? I've thought about it and I'm very confused."

"Now that," says Nyssa, "is a fearless thing to say. I admire that. Truly."

"Hey," says Agnes, warming, "if I knew that all I had to do to get you to be nice to me was hit you with a hammer, I would have done it on the bus."

Nyssa is laughing! "Really, if I am completely honest with myself, I have to admit I was taking things out on you. It's like I started and I couldn't stop." Then her expression changes to dead seriousness. "I'm sorry."

"Thanks," says Agnes. "Now, do you need help with that tray?"

Nyssa appears to be mustering all her strength.

Finally she opens her mouth. "Quack," she says.

The other Mallards give Agnes mystified looks as she huddles with Nyssa at lunch. Agnes just wants to keep Nyssa talking. Both girls sit with one elbow on the table as they talk.

"Did they have to call your mom about your toe?" Agnes asks.

"No," says Nyssa. "I live with my grandfather."

"Oh. Will I meet him at Parents' Day, then?"

"Actually, part of the reason I wanted to go to camp was so that me and him could have a vacation from each other," Nyssa says. "And you know, I just don't want to talk about him if you don't mind."

"Oh, sure," says Agnes, scrambling for another subject. "Well, how about your friends? Are any of them here?"

"My best friend, Rochelle, is actually the smartest girl in school," says Nyssa. "Only she gets horrible grades. And she has a really bad attitude. Except for when she's with me."

"She hates school?" Agnes asks.

"Let's just say we always have a cafeteria table all to ourselves," Nyssa says. "Anyway, she couldn't come here because nobody is going to award a scholarship to a girl like her. It's like, she doesn't have the paperwork to show how brilliant she is."

"You mean, like grades?"

"Yeah. But see, I do have the paperwork. My grades are great. Perfect, actually. So getting the scholarship was easy for me, even though she deserved it just as much. She knows everything about ecology. She is totally into plants and growing things. Her apartment is like a giant agricultural project. She's the one who should be at science camp. It's not fair. As usual."

Agnes realizes with a small jolt that she does not know, or once even wondered, how much camp costs. "Do you miss her?"

"Yes. She's the only girl I've met who cares about the right things," says Nyssa. "If there's one thing I can't stand, it's people that don't care about the right things."

"But come on! She's fun, isn't she? I mean, you must miss other things about her too."

"Fun is not my first priority. But being fair?" Nyssa's eyebrows shoot up. "Now *that's* important."

Agnes's eyes widen. "You know, I've thought about that too!" she says. "People always seem to think that showing off and beating people at everything and . . ." Agnes struggles with putting these strong feelings into words. "It's like putting yourself first is always more important than caring about what the other person feels. Like niceness is weak."

"Do you think it's weak?" Nyssa asks.

"Sometimes," Agnes admits. "People like to bug me about it."

"It's simple," states Nyssa. "All the time, I ask myself: What do *I* really think? How do *I* really feel? And I make myself act on it."

"But the thing is, I really do care about people's feelings. That's who I am."

"Hmm, well," says Nyssa. "Like you said—that's *you*. I'd rather concentrate on what's right."

"Hmm," echoes Agnes as she wonders if, by itself, kindness can be considered "right."

When the Mallards return to work on their soil project, Agnes finds that it's fun to be with Nyssa when she's talking about a subject that interests her.

"Does anybody know why we call this top layer the parent material?" Sandy asks.

"I think it's because it's the parent to all the other layers of soil, right?" Nyssa says, picking up some leaf litter and tossing it between her hands. Then she pauses for a bit and squints at the stuff. "Because if you look at it, it's actually rocks and splinters and broken leaves and things that haven't decomposed really."

"Correct," says Sandy. "When it does get more broken down, you get to this layer." He points to a richer brown ribbon one layer down. "This is called humus soil. It's not quite the stuff a tree puts its roots into yet. But its nutrients drip into these other layers."

"It sort of reminds me of making lasagna," says Agnes.

Sandy chuckles. "That's the first time I've heard that one," he says.

"Tree lasagna," says George.

"And," says Nyssa, "it's a really bad thing to put lead in your so-called lasagna. We have this huge lot by my house no one can build on because it used to be this factory where they painted china plates."

"Yep, old paint used to be loaded with lead," says Sandy. "And that's a sin. Because do you know it takes over a thousand years for nature to make a decent inch of clean topsoil?" He turns toward Beth and Lisette, both of whom are raising their hands. "Girls?"

The one Agnes finally identifies as Lisette-in-the-blue-top swallows hard before she speaks. "We have some garbage buried under where we live," she whispers, as everyone leans in.

". . . and it's turned to gas," adds Beth.

". . . which can explode!" says Lisette. "And for a while it was horribly dangerous!" The twins freeze in a wide-eyed look of alarm.

"With a hellaciously rotten stink too, I'd imagine," says Sandy. "Whew. You never forget it once you smell it."

Agnes can't help but ask, "So, what *does* it smell like?"

A maidenly blush takes over Sandy's earlobes. "Er. . . Well, girls, if you want to know, it's a lot like when someone . . . *passes the crackers.*"

Lisette's nostrils tremble. Beth snorts. Then both the girls dissolve into cackles! Agnes is startled by their bizarre, *loud*, identical goose-honk laughs.

"How long you two been breathing that stuff in, by the way?" Sandy asks.

Lisette and Beth are helpless now, mildly clawing at each other as they honkety-honk.

"Uh-oh," says Kacy, alarmed. "I don't think they're getting enough air!"

"Got *gas*, though," says Rita. "From the exploding lasagna!"

Agnes sees Kacy giggling for the first time. "You're funny, Morris," Kacy says, reaching up to give Rita a playful punch.

Rita grins. "Really?" she says. "Well, thanks, buddy. I'm good at gas jokes, I guess."

"You *were* our school's champion burper," says Agnes.

Willow is smirking. Tiki is beaming.

"Hoo, boy!" Tiki says. "Something tells me it's time for Mallards to get back to the cabin. We've got some brainstorming to do for campfire."

"Cool," says George. "As long as you keep Beth and Lisette away from any open flames."

Agnes is laughing now too, and wondering how her soil-worshiping bunkmate is taking all this.

Nyssa half smiles and shakes her head. "Well, I guess

it's okay to have fun," she says. "In the name of science."

Back at the cabin, Agnes finds herself in the center of a very talkative group of Mallards. The standoffishness of the first day has vanished, and everyone has ideas for Agnes's aquatic life costume.

"I think Agnes should show how toxic our rivers and streams have become," says Nyssa.

"I'm for that," says Agnes. "My T-shirt does say FISH FEVER, after all."

"Yeah," says SPF. "So could she be, like, this giant sea creature trailing garbage behind?"

"Or we could make her hair look like seaweed, and stick a lot of trash in it!" says Rita. "I mean, if you could manage that, Kacy."

"Easy!" says Kacy. "All you gotta do is braid a bunch of sticks in her hair, which would be very simple . . ."

"And maybe stick in some rusted old beer can or something?" suggests Lisette.

"Remember," says Tiki. "We have to find everything around the cabin or in our suitcases."

"No beer cans then," says Beth.

"We have to use my fishing pole," says George. "Don't you think?"

"Yes!" says Agnes. "But not for fishing. Because this is a pollution thing."

"Exactly," says Nyssa. "We're more the fish defender's league here."

"We can just hang a boot or something from the line," says SPF. "That'll show how polluted the stream is."

"Great!" says Tiki. "All fantastic ideas, Mallards!"

Willow slouches to the center of the room. "Except for one thing," she says. "We don't have garbage. Nothin' at this camp is served in bottles, cans, or wrappers. We do that on purpose, you know."

The Mallards digest this for a while. "Doesn't anyone have anything in their duffel bag?" asks George.

"Besides tissue?" says SPF. "I have a little plastic razor."

Agnes pictures razors hung from braids swinging around her face. "Remember," she says, "this is stuff that has to hang in my hair."

"I have a bottle of nasal spray," says George.

After a long silence, Rita Morris leans under her bunk and heaves her duffel to the middle of the floor. She kneels, taking out layers of shorts and shirts and underwear. Finally she yanks open the bag and says, "Quack!"

Agnes peeks inside. "Gee," she says. "There's every kind of gum and candy under the sun in there!"

Rita sighs. "My stash," she says.

"Oh, my," says Tiki. "Were you going to share?"

"I'll share my wrappers," says Rita. Then, sternly, she adds, "The candy has to get me all the way through the month, though."

"Don't worry, Rita" says Kacy, sounding more like the big kid. "We'll just take wrappers. No candy."

Kacy digs in, while Willow directs the other Mallards to get moving. Nyssa runs her hands over the clay layer of this afternoon's soil sample.

"For your cheeks," she says, rubbing the reddish grit over Agnes's face. Then she moves on to her T-shirt and forearms.

"Yeah," says Rita approvingly. "That looks real slobby."

Agnes allows Kacy's little hands to pull her hair into the most uncomfortable formations. The twigs poke her scalp. "Ouch," she says.

"Gotta be strong!" says Kacy, yanking authoritatively. "If I don't pull hard now, your braids will fall apart later."

When Kacy finishes, George and SPF put the fishing pole, now dangling an old tennis shoe, in Agnes's hands.

"Awesome," says Rita.

"Toldja," chirps Kacy, crossing her arms.

Willow and Tiki each take one of Agnes's elbows and walk her to the mirror. Agnes can't believe the transformation. Her new snaky hair does look like trash-choked seaweed. And Nyssa went all-out on her soiling duties. Agnes looks as if she hasn't changed clothes in weeks.

"I'm a walking human garbage dump," she says.

"Oh, Agnes," says SPF, "this costume is so great. I just know you're going to win!"

"Win what?" Agnes asks.

"Tonight's campfire competition!" shouts Tiki. "Let's keep our fingers crossed."

"Wait!" says Agnes. "Exactly how do we win?'"

"Everyone at campfire votes by applause," says Willow.

"It's not a big thing," says George. "It's more of a *pride* thing."

"Some people take it very seriously," says SPF, pointing at George behind her back.

Agnes is glad she didn't realize this before consenting to model.

"Go, Agnes, go," says Lisette sincerely.

"Yay, Agnes," whispers Beth.

"Quack quack-quack!"

"See?" says Tiki. "You got your own cheering section."

Agnes watches the rest of the Mallards leave to take their place on benches by the big roaring campfire. She, herself, is escorted by flashlight to join the other models in an out-of-sight location behind Finney's office.

Agnes tries for a glimpse of Prejean, but it's too hard to see her in the dark among this crowd of girls and boys.

"Okay, kids," Finney announces, "I'm going to pair

you off. When I read your study unit, come up front and meet your co-model."

The first couple called are for Soil Studies. Agnes has to laugh when she sees the girl from Red Squirrels covered in caked-on mud. She's carrying a little sign that says, NOT DIRTY. SOILY! The guy she's paired up with is similarly smeared.

That was an easy one, Agnes thinks.

"Aquatic Studies!" shouts Finney.

Agnes makes her way to the front, careful not to whomp anybody with her tennis-shoed fishing pole. She's joined by a short boy with a cardboard fin sticking out of the top of his head.

"You're a shark, right?" Agnes says.

"Right," answers the boy. "And you would be, what? Miss Rasta Dirt Girl?"

"No. I am a polluted stream full of garbage and sick fish," Agnes says.

"Really?" he says. "I . . . didn't get that."

Uh-oh. Agnes's stage fright begins to kick in. "You really, really had no idea?" she asks the boy.

"Nope," he says.

Before Agnes can panic further, the models are led in a line closer to the campfire. She hears a counselor from the boy's camp announcing the start of the show.

"Good evening! I'm Harley, your host. Welcome, campers, to the wonderful world of eco-couture! Each set of models will take to the campfire catwalk in a demonstration of our study units. After the show, we'll have a contest where you, the audience, vote with your applause."

Immediately, groups of kids begin chanting the names of their own cabins. Agnes notices that some of the voices are pretty deep. *Eighth-grade boys?*

"Nuh-no! It's not like that, kids," Harley says. "We are voting on CREATIVITY! And PRESENTATION! And RELEVANCE TO THE STUDY UNIT! So you guys are going to have to be looking for these things, regardless of whose cabin presents. Understand?"

The crowd shouts in reply.

"First up, I give you Soil Studies. Models are Shawn Levitz from Red Squirrels and Frank Beauman of Timberwolves!"

Finney gives the two a nudge. "Go!" she says. "Once around the campfire, then you can stand to the side and watch the show."

Shawn and Frank give each other embarrassed glances and then walk out together toward the light. Agnes is not prepared for the laughter, cheers, and bellowing. She wishes she could see better what was going on inside that circle.

What Agnes can hear is a foghorn refrain of deep male voices. "FRONK! FRONK!" She figures it must be Frank's nickname. Numanu's Red Squirrels respond with some higher-pitched chants of "Soi-ly Girl! Soi-ly Girl!"

"Next up, Aquatic Studies, brought to you by Agnes Parker of Mallards and Paul Tambini of the House of Moose . . ."

Paul starts walking off by himself. Agnes stumbles to catch up. What a big crowd! Paul holds up his hand in a peace sign as the Moose boom, "Shark At-TACK!" Agnes, feeling wobbly with fear, tries to find the source of the girls' quacks. Finally she spots Nyssa standing up and chanting: "Find the solution! No more pollution!" The other Mallards join in. The volume mounts.

Agnes smiles, relieved. She waves and the Mallards hold up their fists. She blows them a kiss and runs outside the circle to watch the show.

"That wasn't so bad," she says to Paul.

"Yeah," he says. "And we're done."

The models for Outdoor Survival took their turns with tourniquets and slings and blackened eyes. The Trees and Plant Life models were generally covered with leaves. Agnes has a good feeling that the Mallards are really holding their own. Then the next set of competitors are announced.

"Ladies and gentlemen of the campfire, get ready for . . . *Wildlife*! With the Fawns' Prejean Duval and the Eagles' Janssen Driers."

Agnes's mouth opens when she sees Prejean step

into the glow of the fire. She is wearing an oversized brown hooded sweatshirt. *Just* a sweatshirt. With the sleeves pushed up and a leather belt nipping in the waist. Her shiny long legs appear even longer revealed by this makeshift minidress. On her feet she wears someone's brown hiking boots, adding another inch to her height. Two antlerlike branches protrude from her head, tied with those brown and polka dot ribbons.

"ALL *RIIIGHT!*"

"Hey, BOOTS!"

"YEE-HAW!"

The boys are going bonkers over her best friend! Some of them even seem to be making a kind of mating call.

Janssen, also wearing branches for antlers, isn't getting much attention. So he gives up, stops dead in his tracks, kneels, and humbly bows down before Prejean.

Prejean puts her hands on her hips and looks down at the boy. She steps over him in a single stride, shrugs, and sashays off with her head held high. Janssen picks himself off the ground and chases after her.

It is a theatrical exit, and the boys *love* it!

"WOOO! WOOO-HOOO!"

"Na-ture Goddess! Na-ture Goddess!" squeal the Fawns.

Harley finds it difficult to calm the crowd down. When he calls all the duos back to the fire, it isn't difficult to figure out who is going to win the most applause.

Agnes tells herself that she and Paul did okay, maybe second place. But the image she takes away with her that night is that of Prejean Duval, Nature Goddess and Victor, illuminated by fire, clasping her hands together over her head as the crowd of boys shouts her name.

Who was that girl?

CHAPTER SIX

"ABSOLUTELY UNBELIEVABLE," SAYS NYSSA.

It's almost time for lights out, and all of the Mallards except Agnes and Kacy are lying in their bunks, commiserating.

"Yep," says George, clasping her hands behind her head, "those Fawns are *all-l-l* about ecology. Doncha think?"

"Such *creativity!*" says SPF. "And *relevance to the study unit!*"

Agnes stays quiet as Kacy picks the twigs and wrappers from her hair. For one thing, she would feel braggy insisting that she should have won (even though it's true!). For another, she's upset about the implied criticism of Prejean.

"I don't even know why we have to have boys over here," says Rita. "What is the point?"

"Oh, the boys are okay," says George, "when they're not acting like morons."

Finally, Agnes speaks up. "But it's the boys' fault," she says. "Prejean just wore what her cabin came up with."

Rita sits up in bed, her eyes wide. "Prejean!" she says. "Agnes, was that your little grade-school pal?"

"She grew," says Agnes.

Rita lets out a snort. "I'll say."

"Is there . . . any way we can complain?" asks Beth.

Tiki sits cross-legged on her bunk, her chin in her hands. "I understand how you guys feel," she says. "But . . ."

"It will just make us look like a big ole bunch of whiners," drawls Willow. "You know?"

"But what if every campfire is like this?" asks George. "Like some Supermodel of the World contest?"

"I hope not," says Lisette. "It's hard enough for me to get up in front of people."

"Listen, you guys," says Agnes, "Prejean Duval is my best, oldest friend. You can't find anyone more plain old *regular*. Believe me, it would make her completely sick to hear herself called Supermodel of the World."

"Really?" says Rita. "Well, who picked out that costume, I wonder?"

"Well," says Agnes, "Prejean already told me that the other Fawns were extremely . . . fluffy types."

"Speaking of fluffy," says George, "you should see your hair now." She hands Agnes a wet washcloth. "Good luck getting the dirt off!"

Agnes returns to her bunk and starts scrubbing. The conversation momentarily stalls.

"Here's what I think," declares Nyssa.

Agnes looks up at Nyssa's legs dangling from the top bunk and holds her breath.

"We should do nothing."

Agnes lets out her breath.

"But," says Nyssa, "if any more stuff like this happens, then we'll plan a response."

Willow looks concerned. "What did you have in mind?"

Nyssa pauses, and Agnes can see that all the other Mallards lean toward her.

"If we can call upon the same kind of creativity we used here tonight," Nyssa says, "our response can be extraordinarily cool."

"You mean," says Kacy, grinning, "like a surprise or a trick?"

"Or a prank?" says George.

"Yes!" says SPF. "Yes! A revengeful act of art—and science."

The camp's trumpeter blurps out a bungled version of Taps, and Tiki turns out the lights. There is still sporadic giggling in the dark.

"All right, guys," says Tiki. "Let's save the plotting for later."

I don't want to plot, thinks Agnes. And she is still lying with her eyes wide open when the rest of the cabin is echoing with snores.

The next morning at breakfast, Agnes is annoyed to see the Fawns still wearing their silly matching polka-dot ribbons, whispering and laughing, seemingly entranced with one another. The Mallards, by contrast, chew slowly, warily, as they watch the Fawns. Agnes keeps her head down and tries to concentrate on her scrambled eggs.

"Now why can't we girly-giggle like that?" says George dryly. "We definitely need a study unit in girly-giggling. How about you, SPF? You know how?"

"I hear that we're PH-testing soil this morning!" says SPF, breathlessly. "Giggle, giggle, goo!" Her perky expression vanishes. "How's that?" she says.

Nyssa sits with her arms folded on the table, her face the same expressionless mask she wore on the first day. "And notice how a Fawn never goes to the bathroom by herself."

Oh, so what? Agnes was just starting to like her too.

"Really?" asks Kacy. "That's *so* immature!"

"Just watch," says Nyssa.

Sure enough, as one Fawn stands up, three other Fawns do too. Agnes winces when she sees Prejean and Natalie link up, arm in arm, their identical pony-tails bouncing.

"I'll be danged," says Rita.

"I wish I was brave enough to go in with them and spy," says Beth.

Everyone gasps. "That's a great idea!" says Lisette.

Beth lowers her head and blushes as several of the girls send congratulatory quacks in her direction.

"Count me out," says Agnes flatly, still staring down into her plate.

"I'll do it," says Nyssa, standing.

"All right!" says SPF. George gives Nyssa a grateful slug in the arm. But Agnes wonders why Nyssa can't let things like this go.

"Agnes?" It's Beth speaking, but both she and Lisette have their heads inclined together, worried looks on their faces. "Are you okay?"

"No," Agnes says. "I am not."

"She doesn't like us making fun of her friend," says Rita.

"That's right," says Agnes, heating up. "I don't like it. Why pick on other people just to make ourselves feel better?"

"Wow," says George, "you're really upset."

"I promised myself I was going to keep out of this," says Tiki cautiously, "but I think Agnes is right." No one says anything. "Shouldn't we have higher standards for ourselves?"

"Yeah," says Willow. "From what I can see, we're an excellent group of campers. Why can't we just give ourselves credit for what we accomplished last night and drop the rest of this junk?"

Agnes peers at the Mallards' faces. Do they think she's a spoilsport?

After a long pause, SPF raises her hand. "Quack," she says. "I'll go with Tiki and Willow."

George sits, pinching the bridge of her nose. "I guess I'll quack too," she says. "It's hard for me, but I'll do it."

"Quack!" say Beth and Lisette in unison.

"Okay," says Rita, "the Fawns get one more chance. But just one."

"Quack," peeps Kacy. "Me too."

Agnes smiles. "Thanks, you guys. Really."

"No problem," says Tiki.

Agnes feels a tap on her shoulder. It's Nyssa.

Agnes scoots over.

Nyssa slaps her hands on the table. "I'm ready to report," she says.

Nobody clues Nyssa in. Agnes wonders whether she should stop her before she can start. Then Tiki intervenes.

"Nyssa, we've decided that we're going to lay off the Fawns."

"Why?" she asks.

"Because we decided to take the high road," says Willow.

"And we don't want to make Agnes mad either," says Rita.

Nyssa turns to Agnes and lifts an eyebrow. "This is about Agnes?" she asks.

"No, it's not *just* about me," Agnes protests.

"That's good," says Nyssa. "Because if it was, what I overheard in the bathroom would make *you* flip out."

Here we go again, thinks Agnes.

George drops her head in her hands and moans.

"You're killing us, Nyssa," says SPF.

"This is a matter of individual conscience," says Tiki. "I can't tell you all what to do. I can only hope that you Mallards will try to live up to the standards we just tried to set here." She stands and Willow joins her.

"We're meeting in front of the cabin in ten minutes. Okay?"

"Quack," say the Mallards. Most get up to take in their trays, leaving only Agnes, Nyssa, George, and SPF to finish their breakfasts.

As soon as the girls are alone, George says, "Psst! Agnes!" She's grimacing as if she's in pain.

Agnes is immediately concerned. "What, George?"

George peeks left and right, probably to see if anyone is in earshot. "Would you mind if I find out what happened in the bathroom? Like, I promise not to tell anyone else. Even you. I swear."

"You're asking my permission?" asks Agnes. "Boy, I thought you had cramps or something."

"It's worse than cramps," says SPF. "If you try to keep a secret from George, she will obsess about it until she finds out. And she will not only drive herself crazy, she will drive me crazy."

"It's like a sickness," says George.

Agnes looks at Nyssa, who sits impassive, drumming her fingers. "Uh," she says, "I don't want to make you go nuts or anything. Anyway, it isn't up to me."

George gives her hands a single clap. "Thank you!" she says. "You have saved my day!"

SPF rolls her eyes. "And thanks from me too, Agnes."

"C'mon, Nyssa!" George scoots away *like her pants are on fire*, thinks Agnes. SPF tags behind, and turns once to give Agnes another silent *Thank you*.

Agnes takes her time kicking a pine cone all the way back to the cabin. She wonders what it will be like when she and Prejean can be together again. Will she tell her about the Fawn/Mallard rivalry? Will Prejean tell her about whatever was said in the girls' bathroom? Agnes digs her hands into her pockets and gives the pine cone an especially big kick. There, way off by the fire pit, she sees Nyssa huddled with George and SPF.

George seems spellbound. SPF is clapping one hand to her cheek.

As Nyssa gestures, Agnes is sure she hears George say, "Unbelievable!" And SPF seems to be saying . . . "Gag me"?

Agnes stands like a statue until George spots her. She pokes SPF and points at Agnes. Nyssa now sees Agnes as well.

Agnes quickly waves, turns on her heel, and walks off. For the rest of the way she feels a queasy sensation and it isn't until she's back at the cabin that she can pin down what it is. Then she names it:

I want to know too!

The rest of team-building week goes well for Agnes and the Mallards. Agnes tries to stay as friendly with Prejean as she can from a distance. When the Mallards bump into the Fawns during Soil Studies, she waves conspicuously at Prejean just to show her camp buddies where her loyalties lie. Prejean, as it happens, is too busy laughing with a Fawn friend to notice Agnes at first. So Agnes waves harder.

"I don't think she sees you," Nyssa says.

Agnes straightens her arms and crosses them like searchlight beams. She's feeling a little desperate and embarrassed, when Natalie catches sight of her and gives Prejean a nudge. Finally, Prejean returns the wave. Agnes notes that the wave is enthusiastic and happy, but quick, and that Prejean immediately returns to her interrupted conversation. Natalie joins in and all Agnes can see of the two of them are their backs.

Agnes stands there, smarting.

"C'mon, bunk buddy girl," says Nyssa. "We're almost through with this soil notebook. I need your help."

"You need my help?" says Agnes. "With that giant brain of yours?"

"Quack," says Nyssa.

Agnes smiles.

"Are you going to make me quack again?"

"No," Agnes says, laughing. "You're still not a natural quacker."

Nyssa's eyes glint. "And as soon as we're done, we can shoot up some targets with some bows and arrows! Won't that feel good?"

"I want to shoot things!" says Lisette, surprising everyone.

"Me too!" declares Beth.

Agnes and Nyssa give each other a *Who knew?* look.

The Mallards work together, helping each other to identify the makeup of each other's soil samples. Only the twins are left to finish their work.

"We can't figure out what ours is," says Beth, sticking her finger into some dark brown glop.

"I say we just call it mud," says Lisette.

"M-U-D," says Beth, scribbling in her notebook. "We're done!"

Tiki and Willow lead the girls past the diving boards and slides at the water's edge to a place at a safe distance from all the water sports. The archery range has targets set up against thick walls of hay bales. Shafts of light shine down through the tree branches, and the woods look so fresh and green that Agnes imagines this would be a good place to film any movie with Hobbits.

Kacy picks up the bow, and it's almost as tall as she is. "I've never shot an arrow before," she says.

"I have," says SPF.

"She's really really good too," says George. "Show 'em."

SPF takes the bow from Kacy, holds it up with her left hand and threads the arrow with her right.

"Remember, I haven't done this since last summer," she says. She holds her chin level, pulls back the arrow, and *thunk!* It hits in the yellow ring very close to the center.

"Wow," says Tiki.

"Can we try?" asks Lisette.

Bows are handed over to Lisette, Kacy, and Agnes. Agnes listens as SPF cautions them to keep their arms straight, but her aim is wobbly. She closes one eye and tries to aim the arrow tip at the red bull's-eye.

"Don't close your eye!" says SPF. "It doesn't help. Just relax, aim, and let go."

Thwomp! The bow's recoil sends Kacy tumbling on her butt, yet the arrow miraculously sticks in a black outer ring. "Yippee!" she squeals.

Fump! Lisette's arrow narrowly makes it inside the target.

"Good job!" yells SPF, just as Agnes is ready to shoot.

Flink! Agnes's arrow soars over the target, over the hay bales, landing somewhere in the great beyond. "Oof!" she says, wondering what she might have hit.

Nyssa takes the bow. "You are a danger to yourself and others," she says.

"Maybe I could teach Agnes to fall on her butt when she shoots," says Kacy. "It worked for me!"

Willow holds up her hand. "No one shoot!" she says. "I'm goin' to find that arrow."

"Let's all go," says Rita.

The Mallards spread out behind the hay bales. Willow shades her eyes and looks up in the trees.

Agnes keeps walking until she sees the red feather arrow end sticking out of the ground. "Found it!" she calls. When Agnes pulls it from the ground she hears a *clink*. Kicking aside the pile of leaves, she finds a root beer bottle.

"Hey," she says, holding up the bottle as the other Mallards surround her. "I thought we didn't have any trash or bottles or stuff around here."

"Ahem," says George, giving SPF a meaningful look.

Kacy giggles.

"What?" says Agnes.

Kacy quickly covers her mouth. "Uh, nothing," she says.

"The Fawns bring their own trash," says Rita. "And that's all I'm gonna say."

Agnes looks from face to face. "I don't get it," she says.

"Me neither," says Willow.

"Oh, never mind," says SPF. When she motions to the rest of the Mallards to get back to the archery range, they are quick to follow.

"What? Tell me!" Agnes says to Nyssa.

"Agnes, you already told us you don't want to know," Nyssa says.

"Well, now I do want to," declares Agnes. "This is

silly. What am I? A baby? I mean, even *Kacy* knows."

Nyssa stops. "Okay. The bottle? It's for spin the bottle. One of the stupid eighth-grade Fawns brought it with her. This is where they come to make out."

"With who?" Agnes asks.

"With the *boys*," says Nyssa. "After campfire."

Agnes's thoughts go immediately to her best friend. All she can imagine is Prejean sitting glumly on a rock, maybe whispering a sarcastic remark once in a while for the benefit of Natalie Kim. Who would also be sitting on a rock, come to think about it.

"I'm not surprised," Agnes says calmly. "Of course it's easy to believe most of those other girls would do that. But not Prejean."

Nyssa doesn't answer.

"NOT Prejean," Agnes repeats, as much for her own benefit as for Nyssa's. "And she's the only one I know or care about anyway," says Agnes, fully prepared to stare Nyssa down.

"You know what?" says Nyssa, cocking her head.

"What?"

"You are one of the most loyal people I've ever met."

"Oh?" says Agnes, feeling unexpectedly flattered. "Well, thank you, Nyssa."

"And it interferes with your vision of people, you know?" Nyssa states. "But maybe it's something you can't help."

Agnes stops in her tracks. "Really," she says. "Well, *I* don't think I need any help."

"All right. Have it your way," she says.

As the two girls walk, Agnes glances back at the bottle left in the pile of leaves. Part of her wants to go back, pluck it up, and put it in her suitcase. But what message would that send to Nyssa and everyone else? She does trust Prejean, after all. She *does*!

And she plans to keep it up. At least . . . as long as she possibly can.

CHAPTER SEVEN

THE FIRST WEEK AT NUMANU is over and Agnes is already starting to feel like a seasoned camper.

"We're out of the soil now, my friends," Tiki says after breakfast, "and into leaves, grass, and flowers. Plant presses for everyone!" She passes out funny little wooden frames attached to each other with wing nuts.

"We'll collect plants, identify them, and smush them," says Willow.

"Finally," Agnes says. "No offense to soil, Nyssa, but I think this might be more my type of thing."

"And that's not all," says Willow.

"You all are free now!" says Tiki. "Fraternize! Sit

where you want at lunch! Meet your fellow campers!"

"I guess you'll be glad about that, Agnes Parker," Nyssa says with her half smile.

Agnes is not only glad, she's dying to see Prejean. The last time she was separated from Prejean for a whole week was for a family vacation. But something in Nyssa's voice makes Agnes stop and consider.

"Who will you hang out with, Nyssa?" Agnes asks.

"The other Mallards, I guess," says Nyssa. "Don't worry about me. I'm never lonely when I'm alone."

"Well, I don't suppose you'd sit with the Fawns. Would you?"

Nyssa folds her arms. "No," she says.

"Well then, would you mind," asks Agnes, "if I bring Prejean over to eat with the Mallards?"

"You do what you have to do," says Nyssa.

"You sure?"

"Agnes . . ." Nyssa says, sighing deeply.

"Okay, okay," Agnes replies, throwing up her hands. "I'll do what I *want* to do."

Nyssa gives Agnes the *a-okay* sign. "That's better," she says.

"Quack," says Agnes.

Combing the woods and lake bank for native plants, Agnes feels more an artist than a scientist this morning. The lake mist is evaporated, and the sky is a burning blue. Agnes inhales deeply. The air is saturated with that intoxicating, spicy scent of pine pitch. "This just might be one of the most beautiful places in the world," she says to herself.

Agnes finds a vine with tiny purplish flowers and arranges it into the shape of a wreath. After stripping another piece of vine of all its leaves, she makes two initials, PD, and centers them in the plant press.

"That's really pretty, Agnes," Beth says, peering over her shoulder.

"Let me see," says George. She looks in her plant handbook. "That purple flower is called cow vetch."

"Ugly name, pretty flower," says SPF.

"What's PD?" asks Kacy.

"Prejean Duval," says Agnes. "It's a present. I'll give it to her in a few days, after it dries."

"I'm goin' to make one for Tiki," says Willow.

Suddenly, everyone is startled by a shriek. It's Tiki, calling out from a stand of trees. "Quack!" she says. "Emergency!"

Agnes and the other campers rush over to find Tiki pointing at a pretty, three-petaled flower.

"Listen, you guys!" she says. "I told you about nettles and poison oak, but I forgot about this plant. If you run across one of these, please, *please* do not pick this flower. It's called a trillium, and it takes seven whole years for it to bloom from seed." Tiki wipes her brow. "Whew," she says.

"They're actually protected by law," says Willow.

Agnes kneels to study the pale blossom with the little knots in the middle. "It's more like a ghost of a flower than a flower," she observes. "Imagine storing up all your energy for seven years just to push out this little . . . whisper."

"It's so fragile," breathes Lisette reverently.

"I think it's darling," whispers Beth.

The Mallards wander away quietly, almost, Agnes thinks, as an act of respect. She kneels for a while longer, then brushes the pine needles off her palms. When she stands, she finds herself face-to-face with Nyssa.

Nyssa is blinking quickly, and her usual straight line of a mouth is quivering.

"What, what?" Agnes asks, alarmed.

Nyssa holds out her hand and reveals a plucked, white, three-petaled flower. "I killed it," she says. Two fat tears roll down her cheeks.

Agnes puts one hand to her throat. "Ohmigosh," she says.

"I would never intentionally," says Nyssa, swallowing hard, "commit devastating acts of ecological destruction."

Agnes touches Nyssa's arm. "Now, of course you didn't. Oh, don't cry, please," she says. "You didn't know."

"It doesn't make any difference," she says. "I am completely and utterly sickened."

Quacking erupts in the distance. "Lunch!" someone calls.

"Coming!" Agnes shouts.

"I don't care if I ever eat again," says Nyssa. She wipes away her tears with the back of her hand. "Why didn't I check the handbook first?"

"Nyssa," Agnes says, "you're being way too hard on yourself. It could have happened to any one of us."

She shakes her head and wipes another tear. "And I would have been totally ticked off at anyone else who did something this stupid."

"Look," Agnes says, "I'm going to get permission for us to skip lunch today. We can go back to the cabin—"

"NO," she says sharply, straightening up. "Don't do that. You know you want to see your little Fawn friend. I'd . . . I'd rather be alone."

For a few moments, Agnes observes Nyssa in silence. Then she says, "Nyssa, I just can't go off and have fun knowing that you're back here feeling this way all by yourself. So . . . I'm going to have to stay." She cringes a little, waiting for a protest.

Nyssa looks as if she's about to speak, but it's just her mouth quivering again.

"Meet me at the cabin," Agnes says. She runs toward the picnic tables, wondering exactly what she's going to say to get out of lunch. The first Mallard she sees is Rita, exchanging high fives with a group of Red Squirrels.

"Hey, Agnes!" she says. "Come here. I want you to meet these guys."

"Later!" Agnes says. "Looking for Tiki and Willow. Kinda urgent!"

"They're over there!" Rita points toward Finney's office.

Agnes keeps jogging until she spots a group of counselors hanging out by Finney's front door.

"Excuse me," she says. "I mean, quack."

"What's up, Agnes?" asks Tiki.

Agnes gets Tiki to stand off to the side. "I need permission to skip lunch and stay with Nyssa in the cabin."

"Nyssa? Uh-oh," says Tiki. "You guys need to hash something out?"

"Not like that," says Agnes. "She just needs . . . a friend, I guess. You know, like we all do sometime?"

Tiki pats Agnes on the head. "What a good bunkmate you are," she says. "I don't suppose I see the harm— if you stay in the cabin and don't jump on the beds or off the roof or anything."

"We won't!" says Agnes, grateful she didn't have to divulge anything about the murdered flower.

She waves and runs off, but doesn't get far before she hears her name called again.

"Agnes! Yoo-hoo, my dah-ling!"

It's Prejean, standing on tiptoe, smiling like she's about to burst. She skips over to Agnes and gives her a hug. "It's legal!" she says. "We can talk! Come on, I want you at my table today."

Agnes shakes her head. "Oh, man, I wish I could. I really do . . ."

"Got another lunch date?" says Prejean, obviously surprised.

"Just this once I do. It's my bunk buddy. I have to get back to her. It's a long story, but, lunch tomorrow?"

"Tomorrow." Prejean checks her imaginary watch. "I guess I'm free."

"Thanks, Prejean. Now I really gotta go grab Nyssa a sandwich."

"Oh. So long," Prejean says. "I guess."

Agnes feels funny leaving Prejean so abruptly and says a quick sorry before trotting off to the lunch cart.

By the time Agnes reaches the cabin, Nyssa is sitting in the middle of the floor staring at the trillium she has placed before her on a white tissue.

"Hi," says Agnes, panting. "Sorry it took so long."

"S'okay," Nyssa says.

"So, what are you doing?"

Nyssa gives Agnes her level gaze. "I'm apologizing. To the flower."

"Okay. Then what? You want to give it a burial or something?" Agnes asks softly.

"Do you think I should?"

Agnes sits cross-legged across from Nyssa. She stays that way for a while, looking at the flower along with her. "I never would have thought," Agnes says, "that you were so . . ."

"So what?" Nyssa says, her eyes wary.

"I mean, when I first met you, I didn't know you could be crushed or brokenhearted. Especially about a flower. You know?"

"Frankly," says Nyssa, "I'm more likely to be crushed by this sort of thing than, you know, people things. So yeah, you *don't* know me."

"Guess not," Agnes says. She waits again before saying anything else. Dealing with Nyssa right now is a lot like reaching out to pet a strange dog. "About the trillium," she starts, "shouldn't we figure out some way to use it? Burying it seems even more of a waste."

"I've been thinking the same thing," Nyssa says.

"Maybe we could press it," Agnes says. "We could press it and . . ."

"Hang it in the lodge," says Nyssa, awakening to the possibility. "Yes! For future campers. With a note saying THIS IS A PROTECTED FLOWER. And we can tell its story so no one does it again."

"Perfect!" says Agnes. "Except, you know, it's protected by law. So aren't you kind of worried?"

"About being caught?" Nyssa says. "No. I don't even

care if they send me to jail. All I care about is making things right. As much as I can at this point." She stands and fetches her plant press.

Agnes imagines Nyssa behind bars, wearing one of those black and white convict outfits. "You really would go to jail for this flower, wouldn't you?"

"If they made me," says Nyssa.

"And I bet you wouldn't lie about it or try to cover it up or plead insanity either."

"No way," says Nyssa, standing a bit straighter.

"You know, I think you're awesome, Nyssa Vanderhoven," says Agnes warmly. "I really do."

Agnes sees Nyssa blush. "Thanks," Nyssa says. "I mean, quack."

Both girls hold their breath as Nyssa screws down the press. The trillium petals crush down into a perfect triangle. They look at each other and smile.

"This is going to be okay," Agnes says.

"I know," says Nyssa.

When the Mallards get back together after lunch, Willow announces the presentation for tomorrow night's campfire. "We are goin' to do a dramatic interpretation of our first week at camp."

"Meaning?" says Rita.

"A rep from each cabin will stand and say, 'For our first week at camp, the Mallards learned . . . blah blah blah.' You only have to come up with a sentence or two. But you *will* have to face the applause meter again."

"Dang," mumbles Rita. "More creativity."

Kacy wrinkles her nose. "Will the boys be doing it too?" she asks.

"Yep," says Willow. "Tuesday is always group campfire. Only this time, we're goin' to their place across the lake."

"We get to go out by canoe and candlelight," says SPF. "There's singing and everything."

"It's also a social opportunity," Tiki says. "Our brother cabin, the Moose, will be hosting us."

"Will there be . . . slow dancing?" breathes Beth. Lisette chews a fingernail.

"With the Moose?" asks Kacy, paralyzed.

Tiki looks like she's struggling to keep a straight face. "No. There will be no dancing, slow or otherwise."

"Unless one of you guys wants to hootchy-coo around the campfire," says Willow.

"Me!" says George. She throws back her head and undulates around the room.

"Go for it, hula hips," says SPF.

"Yeah. Then maybe if we do that, we can win this time," says Rita.

Agnes ignores this remark. Instead, her attention turns to Nyssa, who is standing now, holding her plant press.

"Can I say something?" Nyssa asks. "I learned something at camp today that I think we can use at the campfire." She gently unscrews the wood frames and motions for the Mallards to look.

"Uh, Nyssa?" says Willow, wincing. "*That* . . . is a trillium."

"No!" says Tiki. She rushes to take a peek. "Oh, dear."

"Nyssa knows," says Agnes. "It was a mistake, Tiki. She picked it before you said anything."

"I also picked it before I read my handbook," Nyssa says. "So it is my fault entirely."

"We were just hoping," says Agnes, "that we could warn everyone about this so it won't happen again. This pressed flower could be hanging up where all the new campers can see it."

"*Before* they study plant life," says Tiki. "Is this why you two ducked out on lunch?"

"Yes," says Nyssa. "I was pretty crushed."

"Actually," Agnes says, "I don't think Nyssa believed that Mother Nature would ever forgive her."

Tiki goes over to Nyssa and throws her comfy arms around her. "I don't know about Mother Nature, but I forgive you."

"Thanks," says Nyssa, stiff with embarrassment. Then she does something that shocks Agnes. She leans in awkwardly, lowering her head until it rests on Tiki's shoulder.

At this, Lisette and Beth spontaneously leap forward and wrap their arms around Nyssa and Tiki. The sight of those two shyest girls, eyes closed and hugging, makes Agnes want to join in. One by one, the Mallards extend their arms and walk forward, until the entire cabin is lumped in an embrace.

"Three cheers for our brave Nyssa!" declares Tiki.

"Quack!" say the Mallards. "Quack! Quack!"

Agnes almost expects Nyssa to struggle loose or plug her ears. But through the tangle of arms and bodies, she can see that Nyssa's eyes are shining.

Chapter Eight

"You know what?" says Willow. "For once, let's just blow off the morning and jump in the lake."

Agnes hopes that Willow isn't kidding. At 7:00 A.M. it's already unbearably hot.

"I'm sticky," says George, pulling her damp night-shirt away from her chest.

"Finney put up a rope swing," Agnes offers. "Yesterday. Anyone hear about that?"

"Mmmm. Rope swing," says SPF dreamily. She reaches for a tube of zinc oxide. Her nose is already deep pink from yesterday's afternoon out in the sun.

Tiki fans her face with her straw hat. "The lake," she says.

"Seriously?" says Willow.

"Why not?" says Tiki. "I'm sure I can fix it with Finney."

"Thank you!" say Beth and Lisette.

"I'm going to wear my swimsuit under my shorts at breakfast," says Kacy.

"Woo-hoo!" says Rita. "I'd jump up and down if I wasn't stuck to my bunk."

Agnes smiles at today's prospects: lazing at the lake, lunching with Prejean, canoeing by candlelight. At breakfast, she raises her hand to give Prejean a salute. Prejean sees Agnes and gives her a funny two-fingered wave.

"What does that mean?" Agnes wonders out loud. And then she sees Natalie doing it too.

"Isn't that dumb?" says George. "The Fawns think that looks like antlers. But it really just looks like they're itching something."

"Let's be fair," insists Agnes. "Is it any dumber than quacking?"

"It's important to be fair," says Nyssa, half smiling.

"Thank you, Bunky," says Agnes.

George and SPF exchange smiles.

"What's so funny?" asks Agnes.

"You two," says SPF. "At first we were so worried for you. Talk about your mismatched campers."

"And you call each other 'Bunky'!" sighs George, mock-romantically. "You melt my heart!"

"Quack," says Nyssa flatly.

"Hey, I'm melting too," says Rita. "Let's swim!"

When the Mallards reach the lake's edge, they throw their T-shirts and sandals in a pile on the bank. Agnes and Nyssa find a safe spot on a rock to leave their glasses. Everyone is in bathing suits except for Nyssa, who wears a tank top and gym shorts from Herbert Hoover Elementary. "I have never worn a bathing suit in my life, and I'm not going to start now," she tells Agnes, apparently quite serious in her no-bathing-suit convictions.

Rita does a running cannonball off the boat deck. When she floats to the top, she splutters, a piece of seaweed dangling in her hair.

"Awesome!" she announces. "It's warm in here already."

Kacy dives in too, while George and SPF climb the ladder to the new rope swing.

"I always wade in," says Agnes. "I hate being cold-shocked." She and Nyssa scoot their feet along the lake bottom, kicking up silt. Both hold up their elbows against the splash as George, bellowing like Tarzan, swings into the water.

"Oh, what the hey," says Agnes. "We're already wet!" She plunges into the water. "Ahh, wonderful!" she says. Floating on her back, she feels she could stay this way forever, drifting, listening to her own breath and staring at the sky.

When Agnes flips over, she can make out a blurry Beth and Lisette. Both are staying in water that laps at their ankles.

"Come on in!" says Agnes. "It's really not that bad!"

Both of them poke each other. Finally Beth speaks up. "Do fish have teeth?" she asks.

"No!" shouts Nyssa. "Not in this lake!"

Beth and Lisette confer with each other. "What about eels?" whispers Lisette.

"No eels!" says Nyssa.

"Turtles?" asks Beth. Both girls refuse to budge.

Nyssa stands up and starts wading toward the twins. Agnes follows.

"I take it neither of you have swum in a lake before?"

"You're right," says Lisette. "We're good swimmers in a pool, though."

"We're used to seeing the bottom," explains Beth. "In a lake, you don't know what's down there."

Nyssa takes Beth by the arm. "Agnes, you take Lisette. We will all get devoured together."

"She's just kidding," says Agnes, tugging at Lisette. "Come on."

Nyssa lifts her bandaged foot out of the water. "Look at how big this splint is. This will be the decoy bait. If any creature wants to chomp, this toe will distract them. Now onward!"

The weird logic convinces the twins. The girls make their way slowly, over the knees, over the hips. They are ready to plunge in over their heads, when they hear what sounds like pounding horses' hooves.

"*Yee-haw!*"

Herds of campers are running toward the lake. Some girls are undressing on the run, stepping out of cutoffs and swinging T-shirts over their heads.

Rita, who is standing on the dock, points and shouts, "Red Squirrels!"

SPF shades her eyes and looks out from the rope ladder. "Welcome, Wood Doves!"

Tiki, lying on her beach towel, looks up from her book. "Finney must've given everyone the morning off."

Before Agnes knows it, there are so many campers in the water that the surface of the lake is rippling like gelatin. The line for the rope swing is backed up around the corner of the deck. Lisette and Beth glide out doing a side stroke.

"I like it better when there's a lot of people in the water," says Lisette.

"More bait," agrees Beth.

Agnes finds that it's hard to tell people apart with her naked eyes. How will she ever find Prejean? "I will return," she tells Nyssa.

There are now many piles of towels and clothes all over the sand. Squinting, Agnes tries to make out where she and Nyssa left their glasses. She blindly makes her way toward a glob of girls. "Hey, did anyone see any glasses? I left mine on top of a rock around here."

She makes her way to another pile of clothing, lifting up everyone's castoffs in search of her covered-up rock. Finally, under a red and white striped towel, she sees the glasses. Grateful that no one sat on them and broke them, she picks up both pairs and puts on her own.

"AGNES!"

Agnes jumps. Prejean is yelling from only three feet away.

"What?" Agnes says, sticking a finger in her ear. "My gosh, you almost broke my eardrum."

"I've been calling your name about forty times!" says Prejean.

"Oh," says Agnes. "I guess I didn't hear you."

"I've been waving. Natalie's been waving. It's like you're in your own little world." Prejean has her well-oiled hand on her hip. Even in a plain navy blue tank suit, Agnes thinks that if she put a flower behind Prejean's ear, her friend would look exactly like a tropical princess.

"Geez, Prejean. I didn't have my glasses on. You know I can't see without them."

"Okay, okay," Prejean says. "I was just wondering why . . . Oh, never mind."

Agnes looks down at Nyssa's glasses in her hands. Now that Agnes can indeed see, she realizes that her bunkmate is no longer in the water. Then she spots her on the sand next to Tiki.

"So, can you come over and say hi?" Prejean asks, pointing at a group of Fawns who are dousing themselves with suntan lotion.

"Um, yeah," says Agnes, distracted.

"What," says Prejean evenly, "do you not want to?"

"Huh?" Agnes says. "No! It's just that I picked up Nyssa's glasses and I got to get them to her before she thinks they're lost."

"Uh-huh," Prejean says.

Agnes drops her hands to her sides. "What is up with you? You're acting weird. Like I'm doing something wrong?"

Prejean puffs out her cheeks. "Your cabin hates my cabin," she pronounces.

Agnes gulps. "Why do you say that?"

"Yesterday we got word through the Red Squirrels that the Mallards hate us and spy on us." Prejean crosses her arms. "Is this true?"

"Well, *I've* never spied on you," Agnes says. Her first instinct is to explain, to calm Prejean down. But there's something about Prejean's attitude that makes Agnes change her mind. "Although we *did* find your bottle," Agnes says. "In the woods. Under a pile of leaves?"

Prejean wrinkles her brow. "And what did you hear about the bottle?"

"We heard that you guys played spin the bottle with those loud doofy boys after last campfire."

Prejean is silent.

"YOU played spin the bottle, Prejean? With the stupid Fawns?"

"YES, I did," Prejean says coldly.

"You did that," repeats Agnes, stunned. "Man. Prejean . . ."

"So now you can't be seen with me because you are so embarrassed in front of your little Mallard buddies?"

"Me?" says Agnes. "*I'm* the one who sticks up for you! Like every day since we got here." She feels herself heating up and clenches her fists. "Honestly. Maybe you are so into your making out and your modeling and your new hairdo that you don't even remember who your real friends are."

Prejean's eyes widen. "Not nice, Agnes."

"Maybe not. Or maybe I just prefer to think about things OUTSIDE of myself. Like about trees and the forests and the world and ecology. THE THINGS WE ACTUALLY CAME HERE TO LEARN ABOUT!"

"I don't have anything to say to that," says Prejean. "Not one thing."

Agnes trembles as Prejean turns and walks away

with that new long stride of hers. "Have fun with Natalie!" she shouts.

When Agnes marches off, pounding her feet into the sand, she feels extra-short-legged, which makes her seethe even more.

As the Mallards prepare for the evening's campfire, Agnes answers the mail her mother sent her, full of happy, excited questions about camp. But she ends up scratching out everything that she writes. How can she explain?

Agnes almost wants to confide in Nyssa about what happened, but doesn't. She does notice that her bunk buddy is quiet, yet always close at hand, writing in a notebook she brought along. Does she sense something's wrong? Agnes wonders.

"Can I ask you what you're writing?" Agnes asks.

Nyssa smiles. "It's a poem about the trillium. For campfire."

"Read it to us, Nyssa?" asks George.

Nyssa pushes her glasses up on her nose, opens her notebook, and sits straight up on her bed. She clears her throat and begins:

Trillium
Count seven years of falling leaves,
of wind and rain and snow,
Seven years of summers—

Before my blossoms show
Leave me where you find me.
For soon, I'll fade away.
But seven years of seasons
are ripe in me today.

"Oh, Nyssa," says Agnes. "How pretty."

Nyssa shrugs. "It's just something I like to do," she says.

"You amaze me," Agnes says.

"It's pretty, yeah," Rita says. "But do you think anyone will know what she's talking about?"

"Rita!" pipes Kacy. "It isn't that hard."

"I got it," says Beth.

"Me too," assures Lisette.

"No, maybe Rita's right," says Nyssa. "I have another one here. Although it is a little darker."

Nyssa flips a page and begins:

Trillium flower, little star,
Dead and gone. That's what you are.
Plucked from bed, the innocent sleeper!
Torn from greenery, death will keep her!
A whole forest feels your lack.
Once you're dead, no coming back.

Nyssa looks up, waiting for a reaction. Agnes tries to come up with a comment.

"Um," says Beth after a long silence, "I like the first one."

The rest of the Mallards quickly agree. A few even quack.

"I guess I'll explain about the flower before I read the poem," says Nyssa. "That way, people will understand it's protected and stuff."

"Good," says SPF. "You've got to be crystal clear. That way even the Fawns and the eighth-grade boys will get it."

Agnes doesn't bother to defend the Fawns this time. "Ha," she says, just to see how it feels.

"Guess what," says Willow. "It's officially my favorite part of the night!" She crawls under her bed and takes out a box of little copper lanterns. "We get to carry these when we canoe across."

Each Mallard takes a lantern and a stubby votive candle.

"It's like a little purse," says Kacy, swinging the box back and forth. "Or Chinese take-out food."

The lanterns are lit, candle to candle, and the group takes off through the woods for the dock. Each cabin divides itself between two canoes. Agnes marvels when all of them are aboard and afloat. With the glow from the lanterns on the water, this night is truly magical.

Tiki starts a song. The girls join in, the paddles dipping to the rhythm:

I see the moon, the moon sees me.
The moon sees the one that I long to see . . .
So God bless the moon and God bless me,
and God bless the one who I long to see.

It's the kind of night that makes you wish for things, thinks Agnes, while gliding and singing. Is there someone Prejean longs to see? she wonders. Some boy she really likes? Agnes felt that way about a boy once. He even liked her back. And Prejean had been totally weird and awkward about the whole thing.

But now that Prejean's beautiful and the boys know it, she jumps into the boy/girl thing all the way—and without Agnes?

And then another thought creeps in that Agnes can't push away. Am I . . . that jealous?

When the Mallards reach the docks at the boys' camp, the Moose are there to greet them. They steady the canoe and help the girls ashore. At first the Mallards are awkward standing there with them. Only the boisterous George seems completely herself, calling them "bro" and giving them trick hand-shakes.

When Agnes sees Paul, the kid she modeled with at campfire, she figures she might be able to come up with something to say.

"Hey, Paul. It's me, Rasta Dirt Girl," she says.

After a second, he recognizes her. "Only you're not dirty anymore," he says.

"It was a costume," she says. "And we went all the way with it."

"Too bad you didn't win," he says. "Because you really should have."

"Thanks," Agnes says. "That's what some of us think."

"Well, the other girls had an unfair advantage," Paul says. "They brought out their secret weapon."

Agnes knows Paul is talking about Prejean and that he's just trying to make conversation. But she can't help but speak up. "That secret weapon? She's my best friend since second grade," Agnes says.

"*That* girl?" says Paul. "You're kidding."

Agnes wants to ask what he means by this, but the counselors from Mallards and Moose start the introductions. First they make all the campers go around and say their names. Then they direct everyone to the campfire.

When the group starts moving, Agnes decides to catch up again with Paul. "Why can't you believe that's my friend?" she asks. "I really want to know."

Paul shrugs. "Maybe because she's kind of a . . . wild one?"

"Explain," says Agnes.

"All right. Last week, a bunch of guys went to meet

a bunch of girls after campfire. They played spin the bottle. When the bottle pointed to your friend, this little scared guy wanted out. He's like this short, little immature kid . . ."

"And?" says Agnes.

"He looks like a nine-year-old, really," says Paul. "Anyway, he wanted to back out, and your friend refused. She actually went up to him and grabbed his T-shirt. Then she pulled him up to a standing position and kissed him like, I don't know. Like she wasn't going to take no for an answer."

Agnes shakes her head. "Impossible!" she says. "There is no way. NO WAY."

"I swear on a stack of Bibles," Paul says.

"Sorry. I'm not calling you a liar. But you have been misinformed," Agnes says.

"Would you believe it if I told you I saw it myself?" says Paul. "Because, actually, I did."

And Agnes just stares ahead as the campfire competition starts. All she can think about is Prejean, her best friend. The skinny girl on the mountain bike, the kid who rolls her eyes and snorts her chocolate milk when she laughs. Agnes can practically see her riding away, waving, growing smaller and smaller. She feels her heart swelling in her chest, thinking: Don't go.

CHAPTER NINE

REVENGE

"SHOULDN'T WE CARRY NYSSA on our shoulders to breakfast this morning?" asks George.

"Not necessary," says Nyssa, running her fingers through her whacked-off hair. "Definitely."

"You're too modest," says SPF. "And you aren't enjoying your victory appropriately."

"Don't you ever bask?" asks George.

"No one ever voted for me before," says Nyssa. "For anything."

"One thing we know now," says Agnes, "is that if there ever was any serious Fawn bias, it's over now. Otherwise, they'd have won last night too."

"I never *didn't* like the Fawns," says Lisette, tucking the blanket in around her bunk.

"I'm not that nice," Rita says. "I'm glad we beat 'em."

"And only because we beat 'em," George says, smiling, "I hereby promise to be as fair and generous as Agnes from now on."

"Yay, Agnes!" echoes Tiki. "You have been exceedingly well-behaved throughout the entire Mallards/Fawns controversy."

"Excruciatingly well-behaved," mumbles Nyssa.

Agnes reddens. She knows exactly what Nyssa is saying. *I'm just good at not making waves.*

"I'm glad that's settled," Willow says. "Now is everyone ready to face the day?" She opens the door and steps outside. One of her flip-flops sticks and she almost trips. "What the . . . ?" She shakes her foot. "Yuck! I'm stuck!"

Agnes hurries to the open door and watches as Willow puts one hand on top of her hat and gazes up and down the front of the cabin, disgust written all over her face. "You have got to be kidding!" she says.

Agnes steps out onto the threshold before Willow can say "Don't!" Her tennis shoe is stuck in a deep puddle of dirty honey. Beth and Lisette, following close, step in the stuff, too shocked to make a sound. SPF and Kacy bump into the twins, and back against the honeyed doorsill.

"My HAIR!" shrieks Kacy. A wad of light brown hair is slapped to her right cheek like adhesive.

"I'm gonna kill!" hollers SPF, lifting a shoe out of the muck.

"You guys!" Willow yells. "DO NOT touch anything else when you come out of the cabin."

Agnes hops down from the doorstep and turns around.

"Ohmigosh." The entire front of the cabin is honey-smeared and stuck all over with wads of pine needles. Clumps stick out from the windowsills like stickpins. Fistfuls are plastered in bumps over the Mallards sign. Honey drips from the top of the door.

George and Tiki hop outside. "Gross!" declares George. "This place looks like a dying porcupine."

"Or a cabin that grew fur," says Tiki.

Beth and Lisette lean on each other and gasp. "Doesn't honey attract bears?" asks Beth.

"It's already attracting flies," says Willow.

Rita finally stumbles out, scowling and grinding her teeth. The rest of the girls are quiet as she grumbles, her face turning from white to blotchy red. "Dirty pondscum-sucking *Fawns!*" She pounds her fist into her palm with a smack.

"Rita," says Tiki. "We're done with that, remember?"

"Who *else* would it be?" Rita asks.

"Maybe we should see if other cabins are hit first," says Agnes.

On the way to the lodge for breakfast, the Mallards find all the other cabins to be untouched. Even the Fawns' place looks empty and undisturbed.

"Wait here," calls Rita, jogging up to the Fawns' front door.

"There's no one there!" cries Kacy.

"Duh!" says Rita. She jiggles the door handle, looks around the threshold, glides her hand over the door-jamb. "A-ha!" she says, rubbing her fingers together. "Sticky!"

Kacy runs over and touches the sticky spot. "Yep," she says, "that's honey."

"And look down here," says George, pointing down to the dirt. "If this isn't pitch . . ."

She picks up a glob and sniffs. "It's honey!"

"That's it!" says SPF. "At breakfast, I'm checking their shoes. They must have dirt and honey all over themselves."

Agnes wanders over to the side of the cabin and can't believe what she sees. "Never mind the shoes," she says. She directs the Mallards to her find: five pairs of wet tennis shoes drying on a log. One of the pairs is definitely Prejean's.

"Does this kind of thing happen at camp a lot?" asks Beth.

"At least once a season," says Willow.

"But don't go planning your revenge, girls," Tiki

says. "All this means is that we counselors are going to have a big meeting tonight. Finney will want to nip this in the bud."

"I don't know why they'd hate us so much," says Lisette, looking stricken. "What did we ever do to them?"

"Is this just because we beat them last night?" says Beth.

Agnes is taking the cabin-trashing personally. Prejean took part in this! Right after their fight. "I know why," says Agnes.

"It's because they're sore losers," says George.

"Partly," says Agnes. "But it's also because someone from the Red Squirrels told them that we don't like them."

All eyes turn to Rita.

"What?" she says. "So this is my fault?"

Nyssa, who has been quiet so far, says, "Can I make a suggestion? How about we just keep our cool"—she subtly shifts her head toward Tiki and Willow—"and *wait*."

George looks toward the counselors, then her eyes light up. "Yeah, yeah," she agrees quickly.

"No need to act any differently at breakfast," Nyssa continues.

"I get you," mumbles SPF. "Anyone hungry?"

"I sure am!" squeaks Kacy.

The entire group departs for breakfast in an exaggeratedly normal mood, as if they had nothing more on their minds than pancakes.

"What is everybody looking for?" Agnes whispers as soon as she gets Nyssa alone.

"We're keeping our eyes out for *opportunities*," murmurs Nyssa out of the side of her mouth.

"But Tiki and Willow said—"

"Tiki and Willow said they'll be out at a big counselors' meeting tonight," Nyssa says. "Now let's just zip it 'til then."

At first Agnes resists the revenge vibe glinting in all her fellow Mallards' glances. But after a morning on the bucket brigade, rinsing the sticky sludge from the cabin with brooms and water brought all the way in from the lake, *not* participating in revenge starts to sound absurd.

That afternoon during Aquatic Studies, as the Mallards collect pond water with eyedroppers, Willow and Tiki walk out of earshot.

"Do you think we should sneak honey from the lodge this evening?" whispers Kacy.

"Nah," says Rita. "We have to do something completely different. Otherwise we look . . ."

"Like we can't come up with any good ideas on our own," says George.

"Tiki's coming!" whispers Beth, panicking.

"Shhh!" says SPF.

As a distraction, Agnes heaves her collecting jar in the pond near Beth's foot. "OOPS! Can you help me with that?" Agnes says.

"Sure," says Beth, bewildered until she sees Agnes wink.

"I'LL GET IT," says Lisette, as if reading badly from a cue card.

"Do you ever get the feeling," says Agnes, edging over to Nyssa, "that Beth and Lisette have *never* done anything sneaky before?"

"I predict this whole episode will be extremely stressful for both of them," Nyssa says seriously. "Yet healthy in the long run," she adds.

"Actually, I'm kind of concerned about how easy this is for *me*," Agnes says. "Because usually I'm not into making trouble."

"Really? No!" says Nyssa. "And here I had you pegged as this total *rebel!*"

"Funny," says Agnes. "Very funny. But you know, it's weird for me, in a different way than it is for you guys. Not just because I'm a chicken. Which I sort of am. But because of Prejean."

Nyssa and Agnes step farther down the bank.

"It's interesting that you call yourself a chicken, Agnes Parker," says Nyssa. "That's extremely honest of you."

"I don't know if it's honesty, exactly . . ."

"No! It is. I think that you are really coming around.

You are admitting that you're a little on the wimpy side. Which is much better than hiding behind fake-y integrity."

Whenever Agnes thinks of the word *integrity,* she pictures some old guy in a black-and-white photograph with a bowtie and a pocket watch. "You think that I'm full of, um, fake-y integrity?"

Nyssa pauses. "First, let me ask you a question," she says. "Don't you ever feel the slightest bit fake when you stick up for Prejean? I mean, aren't you actually mad at her? *Yet?*"

All Agnes has to do is remember the shock of seeing Prejean's sneakers drying on the log. "I am mad now."

"Then if you act any other way than mad, that's fake." Nyssa shrugs. "It's pretty simple."

Agnes thinks this over and tries to find the sense in it. She contrasts herself to Nyssa, and wonders if integrity is cowardly, or maybe just something teacherly and boring. Or just plain insincere.

Silently, Agnes vows to watch herself for signs of too much integrity. The fake-y kind, anyway. "I'm also creative," she volunteers. "I don't know if you've noticed that."

"Creative is good," says Nyssa.

"Artistic, actually," Agnes says. "And I have lots of good ideas."

"Cool," says Nyssa.

"You'll see," Agnes says.

"Ah," says Nyssa. "The rebel plots."

Before dinner, Agnes sneaks over to the Fawns' cabin. Terrified of being spotted, she's careful to hide behind trees. She spies the tennis shoes, still drying on the log. *Grab them!* she dares herself, then quickly realizes that there's no way to carry five pairs of tennis shoes by herself through the woods unseen.

Tiptoeing around the back of the cabin, she spots some bathing suits and underwear hung on a makeshift clothesline to dry.

A-ha!

Agnes holds her breath and scrambles out from behind her tree. Fear is making her feel unusually clumsy and she forces herself to slow down, carefully grabbing each suit, panty, and bikini bottom from the line. Then she wads them, sticks them under her T-shirt, and runs back to the Mallards.

The first people she sees from her cabin are Lisette and Beth, sitting on the stoop playing a game of cards. They look up at Agnes and then at her bulging T-shirt. "What have you got in there?" asks Beth.

"Come around back!" says Agnes. "Right away!"

"Hey, what's up, Agnes?" booms Rita from the doorway. "You look like Santa Claus."

Agnes puts her finger to her lips and points to the back of the cabin. Rita nods and grabs Kacy.

"Look here," says Agnes when Rita, Kacy, and Nyssa arrive. She pulls out her wad of semi-damp clothes. One of the bikini bottoms drops in the dirt. Agnes picks it up with a thumb and forefinger.

"Eww," says Kacy. "Who do these belong to?"

"The Fawns!" Agnes says. "Just ripped 'em off the clothesline."

"What are you going to do now?" asks Lisette. "Hide them?"

"We could," says Agnes. "Or I figure we can come up with something tonight."

Kacy tugs Agnes's sleeve. "You did good, Agnes," she says. "Real good."

"Did I?" she says.

"Welcome to the dark side," says Rita, rubbing her hands together. "Mwha-ha-ha-ha!"

"Thank you," says Agnes, taking a little bow.

"You did that all by yourself," Nyssa whispers.

Agnes thinks she detects a note of actual admiration in Nyssa's voice. "I told you," she says, tapping her head. "Idea person."

When Tiki and Willow finally leave for the counselors' meeting, the mood in the cabin is decidedly upbeat.

"Have a good meeting, you guys!" says George, with even more spunk that usual.

Agnes thinks everyone must look like cartoon cats

with feathers sticking out of their mouths, but Willow and Tiki leave without any questions.

"Have a good time!" SPF calls after them as George smiles angelically. The girls stay silent for a good thirty seconds, listening for sounds outside.

"All right! Bring out the underwear!" cries Rita, diving under Agnes's bed. She drags out the duffel and kicks it over to Agnes.

Agnes unzips the bag and removes the clothes, including the bikini bottom that fell in the dirt.

"What happened to that pair?" asks George.

"Dropped them," says Agnes. "Pretty disgusting, huh?"

"Hee!" says Kacy. "Maybe we should do that to all of them."

"And hang them back on the clothesline," says SPF, laughing.

"Too easy," says George. "All they'd have to do is swish them around in the lake to get them clean. I want them to have to work like we did."

Beth and Lisette are sitting on their bottom bunk, raising their hands.

"We might have a good idea, we think," says Lisette, eyes shiny.

"Yes!" agrees Beth, almost loudly.

"Tell," says Nyssa.

"Well," says Beth, "Lisette and I do a lot of baking. Plus we do a lot of cake decorating too."

"And it would be the easiest thing in the world to take a plastic bag, like a Ziploc bag?" says Lisette. "You can cut a little corner on the edge. And just squeeze . . ."

"What she's saying is we could decorate the panties. With a pastry bag," Beth says.

"I don't get it," Nyssa says.

"You mean," asks Agnes, "with frosting?"

"Oh, no!" says Beth. "We don't have frosting."

"But," says Lisette slyly, "we do have a lot of chocolate we could melt."

"But that's up to Rita," says Beth quickly.

Rita crosses her arms. "Oh no you don't," she says. "I'm running low as it is."

"Well, I think Beth and Lisette are brilliant," says George. "Chocolate-filled bikini bottoms, hanging from a clothesline. It's gross, annoying, *and* messy."

"I love the idea too," says SPF. "Oh Morris, come on. For the Mallards? Please pretty please?"

"No," Rita says. "Besides, how are we going to melt chocolate? We can't sneak into the kitchen. There's no sun out anymore."

The Mallards sit with their chins in their hands.

Then Agnes says, "I got it. Put chocolate pieces in a plastic bag. Then put the bag in under the covers with one of us. Our body heat can melt it."

"It'd be like a chicken hatching an egg!" says Kacy.

"I'll be the hatcher!" says George. "Rita, you got to let us."

"And Rita," Agnes adds, "you don't even have to give up any candy. I promise, I will put a postcard in the mail first thing tomorrow. On Parents' Day, I guarantee you that my mother will bring a ton of replacement chocolate."

"Well," says Rita, softening. "I could really use some peanut M&M's."

"No problem!" promises Agnes.

"All right!" says Rita. "Deal!"

"Quack!" says Agnes.

In minutes, Lisette and Beth have broken up several Hershey's bars and put them in a plastic bag. George crawls onto her bunk, and the Mallards heap her with all of the blankets in the cabin.

"Just hold the bag under your armpits," Agnes says. "I'm afraid if you lie on it, it'll splurt all over."

"Yeah, careful," says Rita. "'Cuz I'm not giving up any more chocolate."

In about ten minutes, George emerges from the bedding sweating and holding a bag of mushed-up chocolate.

"I wouldn't eat that sludge if you paid me," says SPF, laughing. She picks up a pair of underwear from the floor. "Oh, my!" she says, stretching the elastic. "You better c'mere, Agnes."

Agnes sees PREJEAN DUVAL written in neat, tiny letters inside the waistband. Briefly, she pictures Mrs. Duval with her reading glasses and her laundry marker, toiling under a bright light in the Duvals' den on a summer evening. But then she pictures Prejean, smearing the Mallards' front door with honey and hurling fistfuls of sticks and pine needles.

"I'll do the honors," Agnes says.

Agnes holds the bag as Lisette pokes a corner with a pencil. She squeezes and the chocolate oozes out like toothpaste. Plop! Plop!

Then Rita comes out of nowhere and slaps the underwear between her hands as if popping a balloon. The Mallards squeal. "Gross!" yells Agnes, jumping back. Splurts of chocolate go flying out the leg holes.

"Ick! That is so disgusting!" cries Kacy, holding her stomach. "It looks like you smashed you-know-what in there."

George and SPF are bent over, cackling uncontrollably. Beth and Lisette both stand with their hands over their mouths, shaking with giggles. Suddenly, everyone wants a turn at chocolating. When all the clothing is splattered and as gross as they can get it, Nyssa volunteers to hang the load back on the line.

"Anyone want to come spot me?" she asks.

Agnes steps forward. "I will," she says resolutely

Rita finds there's a bit of chocolate left over in the bag and she insists that Agnes take it with her. "For the tennis shoes!" she says.

The rest of the Mallards hurry to remake the beds and clean up all traces of spattered Hershey's bars as Nyssa and Agnes step outdoors under a full moon.

"We better not talk until this thing is over," says Nyssa. "In and out. That's how we're going to do it."

"Yes! My lips are zipped," says Agnes. The girls nod good luck and, grinning, skulk out into the moonlit forest.

Agnes slips her finger into Nyssa's back belt loop, careful to match her every footstep. When they reach the Fawns', both girls crouch behind a tree, breathing quietly, straining their eyes in the dark to make sure the coast is clear.

Nyssa turns to Agnes and gives her the okay sign. The girls tiptoe forward, careful not to make crinkly noises with the bag, when the bushes stir and . . .

"GOTCHA!"

Agnes can't see anything except a bank of flashlights beaming in her eyes. "Shhhhooot!" she hisses through her teeth. Nyssa says something worse. Then both drop their bags, raise their hands, and surrender.

CHAPTER TEN

Dear Mom and Dad:

Before I tell you anything else, I want to tell you this: Nyssa Vanderhoven and I have spent the entire morning cleaning the showers and latrines with old rags. Then we swept the dining hall and refilled all the salt and peppers and ketchups and mustards. Followed by peeling 4 million oranges. Followed by dinner dishes and more sweeping. And more stuff I've left out in between.

So anyway, as you can guess, I am being punished. I squirted chocolate in Prejean's underwear and a bunch of other girls' bathing suits. But they totally deserved it. And I don't even think I'm sorry. But I do feel bad.

I can hardly wait to see both of you and talk to you on Parents' Day.

Love, Agnes

P.S. I told the girl I took the chocolate from that I'd replace it. Can you bring five Hershey's bars no nuts and a pack of peanut M&M's? Or would that be aiding a criminal?

Agnes feels a hand on her shoulder. "You tired?" George asks.

"Ex-hausted," says Agnes.

"I still don't know why you guys took all the blame," says George. "It was great of you, I know. But we would have stood up for you."

Nyssa, who has been lying flat on her back, raises her head. "We know that. That's why we did it."

"I can't believe that the Fawns turned you in," says Rita. "After all the stuff they did to us."

"We didn't have real proof," says SPF. "So it was a perfect checkmate."

"Yeah. But to ambush you from the bushes?" says George. "They're the ones who started this whole thing."

"If you guys could have held out for just one night," says Willow, "we would have warned you. Finney told us she will take no prisoners on this issue."

"She took *us* prisoner," grumbles Nyssa.

"We're the examples," says Agnes. "Sabotage season

is officially over." She rests her head in her arms. When she closes her eyes, she can still see the shadows of Prejean, Natalie, and the rest of the Fawns surrounding her with flashlights.

"We shouldn't have tried to top them," says Lisette

"Here is your mantra for the day: *Guilt is a useless emotion*," intones Nyssa.

"We can't help it," says Beth.

"This is probably harder on you two because it's your first adventure in revenge," Nyssa says. "Believe me, it gets easier. Look how long it took Agnes to get back at Prejean. Now I bet she'd do it again at the drop of a hat. For good reason too."

This makes Agnes wince. "No, I wouldn't," she says.

"Agnes," says Nyssa in a warning tone, "don't backslide! You know very well that there's no sticking up for that girl anymore."

Agnes doesn't say so, but no matter what, she could never think of Prejean as just "that girl."

The Mallards cling together for the rest of the week. Agnes tries not to look anywhere in Prejean's direction. Sometimes she imagines that Prejean is watching her, hoping some kind of friendly acknowledgment. But there's no way to know without looking, and she refuses to be caught looking first.

On Sunday morning, the girls are up early showering

and sprucing up the cabin. Afterward, as they set to work making pine cone place holders for the Parents' Day lunch, Nyssa writes in her notebook instead.

Agnes has been careful not to ask too many questions about Nyssa's family. Still, it seems unfeeling not to say anything at all this morning.

"Look, Nyssa," says Agnes, trying to be playful. "I have two parents coming. You're welcome to either Rosemary or Jim." She holds up her completed pine cones. "I'll take whoever's left over."

Nyssa looks up from her notebook with her old steely stare. She says, "No thanks."

George, who catches Nyssa's glare, gives Agnes a sympathetic look. "Hey, Nyssa," says George, "how about you sit with me and my mom and my annoying aunt?"

Nyssa keeps writing.

"Do you think your grandpa might come?" asks Kacy.

"Nope and nope," says Nyssa. "And if you don't mind, I don't need to talk about this. Believe me, I'm fine." Nyssa scowls and continues scribbling.

"She's ours this afternoon," says Tiki. "Mine and Willow's. Actually, we are very much looking forward to being Nyssa's special guests."

Agnes sneaks a look at her watch. She doesn't want Nyssa to know, but she can hardly wait to see her own parents.

"I hope your glue is dry," says Willow, "because it's time to set up the tables and greet your folks!"

By the time the Mallards get to the lodge, there's already a large crowd of parents milling outside Finney's office. Agnes helps everyone set the table as quickly as possible. When she finally spies her parents standing side by side, chatting away, she's fairly bursting with impatience.

All at once, the Mallards hear an extraordinarily loud *haw-haw* echoing through the woods.

Haw-HAW-HAW!

"Wow," says George. "Do you guys hear that?"

"It's sort of a donkey laugh," says SPF.

"Haw-haw-haw! HAW-haw-HAW!"

Agnes sees the source of the Haw-ing. It's a man in a bright green T-shirt and brown plaid slacks. He's slapping Agnes's dad on the back. "You got it, Jim!" he brays.

"No," says Nyssa.

"What's up, Nyssa?" asks Agnes. She sees that her bunkmate's face is ashen.

Nyssa, frozen at first, looks left and right, turns, and breaks into a dead run deep into the forest.

"What in the world . . . ?" says Agnes. "NYSSA!" she shouts.

The other Mallards, led by Willow toward their waiting parents, don't notice. But Tiki, still at the rear, runs after Nyssa. Agnes, bewildered, wonders if she should go too. But the sight of her mother and father standing there is too powerful a draw.

"Mom! Dad!" Agnes waves.

Her mother looks up from her conversation with the plaid-slacks man and waves back. "Hey, honey!" she shouts.

In moments, Agnes is folded in her mother's arms. Her father leans over and kisses the top of her head.

"Look how golden you are," says Mrs. Parker.

"I've been spending a lot of time at the lake," says Agnes.

"So you *do* get out," Mrs. Parker says. "I'm glad it hasn't been all about cleaning the latrines."

"Latrine cleaner, are you?" says the plaid-slacks man. "I was just telling your mom here that I could probably save this camp one-third on its entire soap and chemical surfactant budget. Not only THAT, but you could turn around and make that money and then some selling it yourself!"

"We'd like her to finish seventh grade before she goes into chemical sales, I think," says Mrs. Parker.

"Well, maybe," concedes the man. He jerks a thumb toward Agnes's dad. "But Jim here, he can start out selling on the side. Because I'm telling you, this stuff sells itself."

Agnes watches as her father's eyebrows raise ever so

slightly above his glasses. "What are you going to sell, Dad?" Agnes asks.

"Honey," says Mrs. Parker quickly, "this is Mr. Vanderhoven. Mr. Vanderhoven, this is Agnes."

"What?" says Agnes, immediately realizing how shocked she sounds.

"I'm trying to get your parents to call me Bill," he says brightly.

Agnes looks into the man's face and immediately notices Nyssa's steel-gray eyes.

"I was telling Mr. Vanderhoven that I think you and his granddaughter are bunk buddies," says Mrs. Parker.

"That's right," says Agnes. It's the smile that's different, she thinks. It strikes her as the kind of grin that never stops.

"So you are Noreen's friend! Well, I'll be darned," says Mr. Vanderhoven, giving his hands a clap.

"Actually, we've been calling her Nyssa," says Agnes.

"Well, her name is *Noreen*," says Mr. Vanderhoven. He looks over his shoulder. "Where is she, by the way?"

Agnes feels herself redden. *Think, think . . .*

"I brought her a present," he says, showing Agnes a paper sack with a stick-on bow.

"She's . . . in the cabin, I think," Agnes says. "She didn't know you were coming. So she decided to skip lunch."

Mr. Vanderhoven smiles—a bit shakily, Agnes thinks. "I wonder why she thought that," he says.

"I'll go look for her. Okay?"

"Okay!" says Mr. Vanderhoven. "Me and Rosemary and Jim'll just visit."

"I'll hurry," Agnes says.

When Agnes gets close to the cabins, she begins to shout Nyssa's name, briefly wondering if she should try shouting "Noreen." Hoping to catch Nyssa at the Mallard cabin, Agnes sneaks up and bursts in the door.

Tiki is standing there, holding up a piece of notebook paper. "Look at this," she says.

TELL HIM I'M SICK.
NYSSA

"That's her grandfather she's talking about," says Agnes. "He's here. I just talked to him."

Tiki sits on her bed. "Oh, my gosh."

"He really wants to see her," Agnes says. "What should we do?"

"I gotta keep looking for her."

"But what if you can't find her?"

Tiki shakes her head. "Then I'm going to have to tell her grandfather she ran away. And Finney too. This isn't a secret that's mine to keep."

"Yeah, I guess not," Agnes says. "Listen, I have to go

back. I'll tell Mr. Vanderhoven you're looking. And I'll keep my fingers crossed."

When Agnes catches up with her parents and Mr. Vanderhoven, the Parents' Day barbecue has started. There are lines at the chuck wagon, but the Parkers are waiting at the Mallard table with Nyssa's grandfather.

"Hey," says Agnes, trying to look optimistic.

"Where's our girl?" asks Mr. Vanderhoven.

"I talked to our counselor," Agnes says, "and she's trying to find her."

Mr. Vanderhoven blinks a few times. "Well, she couldn't just disappear, could she?"

"Of course not," says Mrs. Parker.

Other parents join the Mallard table, taking their places at their appointed pine cones. All of them are carrying trays of grilled hamburgers or tofu hot dogs.

"Shall we go stand in line?" asks Mr. Parker.

Mr. Vanderhoven taps his fingers on the table. "You go ahead," he says. "I'll wait here for Noreen."

Agnes tugs on her mother's sleeve. "Let's go! Right now. Aren't you hungry?" She pulls at her father too.

"What's going on?" Mrs. Parker whispers as they leave the table.

Agnes launches into her explanation of the mystery of Noreen/Nyssa. "She was so sure he wasn't going to show up," Agnes says. "She never wrote or invited him."

"Does anybody have any idea where she might hide?" Mr. Parker asks.

"Tiki's looking right now," she says. "I feel so terrible. What if she can't find her?"

"Oh, dear," says Mrs. Parker. "Is Tiki the girl with the pom-pom hat?"

"Yeah," says Agnes.

"She's over there now," says Mrs. Parker.

Agnes watches as Tiki, accompanied by Mrs. Finney, approaches Mr. Vanderhoven at the picnic table. He smiles, vigorously shakes their hands, and follows them to the shade of a nearby tree. He keeps smiling as Tiki hands him Nyssa's note, which he reads and quickly tucks into his pocket.

Agnes watches Finney put her hand on his arm, incline her head, and look into his eyes. They walk slowly toward Finney's office. And that's the last Agnes sees of Mr. Vanderhoven on Parents' Day.

CHAPTER ELEVEN

THE PARKERS SPEND MOST OF their time talking about the missing Nyssa. It isn't until late in the afternoon that Agnes spots Mr. and Mrs. Duval in the distance. Prejean is obviously telling them a funny story. She's using her familiar big gestures. And as she always does, Mrs. Duval tucks in her chin when she laughs.

Watching the scene makes Agnes feel a kind of homesickness. And then she senses that her mother is watching her.

"Let's go say hi to the Duvals," says Mrs. Parker.

"Oh Mom, I just can't," Agnes says.

Mrs. Parker strokes Agnes's back. "Now, honey. I'm

sure that Mrs. Duval is big enough to forgive any and all underwear damage."

"It's not just that," Agnes says. "It's Prejean, and how everything's way too . . . screwed up."

She tries to explain how she and Prejean have grown apart without mentioning the making out subject, and ends up talking a lot about Natalie Kim.

"So are you saying that Natalie and Prejean found they have a lot in common?" asks Mrs. Parker.

"Well, yeah," Agnes says. "At first I think they felt like outsiders together. Everyone was asking them about racial stuff, which really doesn't happen at our school, you know."

Mrs. Parker turns serious. "And what do you mean by racial stuff?"

"Not bad stuff, really," says Agnes. "Just more like curiosity."

"Hmm," says Mr. Parker, looking over at his wife. "Agnes, did you ever think that maybe Prejean may be having a harder time? Outside the bubble of our neighborhood, I mean?"

Agnes stiffens. "Well, you're talking about her race, obviously. But I've never cared about junk like that."

"We understand," Mrs. Parker says. "But you should realize that there's probably a whole lot of things that Prejean is going to have to deal with out in the world that you won't have to."

"Oh, it isn't like that, Mom," says Agnes. "Prejean's so-called problem is she's totally beautiful! Honestly, *that's* the thing that nobody can get over around here."

Mrs. Parker puts her arm around her daughter's shoulders. "That may be true. But maybe you could keep an open mind? Really, who knows what she's going through right now? Especially now that you two aren't talking."

"Actually," says Agnes, "the only thing I heard about Prejean's race is . . . that she isn't black *enough.*"

Mrs. Parker opens her eyes wide. "And don't you think there's something a little ugly in that statement?"

Suddenly, Agnes really doesn't want to talk about this subject anymore. In fact, she has never wanted to talk about it. It makes her feel creepy discussing Prejean, her almost-sister, as some alien life form.

"Oh," Agnes says, "I don't even know what a remark like *not black enough* means! It's just too stupid. In fact, I'd rather just . . . stop talking about it."

Mrs. Parker takes a deep breath. "Well, dear," she says, after a pause. "If you want to drop this for now, I understand. As it is, your dad and I have a long drive ahead of us, I'm afraid."

"Are you sure it's okay if we leave now?" asks Mr. Parker. "I was hoping to get home in time to finish some drawings before tomorrow morning."

"I know," Agnes says. "It's okay." She hugs him.

"Your dad is so busy lately," Mrs. Parker says. "And then there's that new part-time soap-selling business of his."

"Did I commit to soap?" asks Mr. Parker. "Mr. Vanderhoven was very persuasive."

"No, Dad," Agnes says. "You were just being nice."

When Nyssa finally returns to the Mallards' cabin, the parents have already gone home—including Mr. Vanderhoven.

Willow, who has been standing outside on Nyssa-watch, spots her first. Tiki hurries out to join them, shutting the door behind her.

"Boy," says George. "Don't you want to eavesdrop on that conversation?"

"Did anyone see her face?" asks SPF.

Agnes wishes she had. She would love some kind of clue to how and why Nyssa did what she did.

The door opens. "All right," says Willow. "I want you all to know that Nyssa's safe and sound."

"Is she coming in?" asks Lisette.

"Tiki's takin' her to Finney's," says Willow. "We promised we'd call her grandfather when we found her."

"Are they going to let her stay?" asks Beth.

Willow scratches her chin. "I don't know," she says.

"No!" Agnes says. "Willow, you can't mean that."

"Running off like she did is a big deal, Agnes," says

Willow. "We had a bunch of counselors lookin' for her. Finney called the Forest Service."

"But we knew she was coming back," says Agnes. "Didn't we?"

"We assumed she would," says Willow. "But we had to take precautions."

"Is there any way we can make a case for her to stay?" Agnes asks.

"Like I said," replies Willow. "We'll have to see."

An hour later, Tiki returns alone. She plops down on her bunk. "Finney decided to keep Nyssa in her quarters overnight."

"I'll bet Nyssa is scared of her grandpa," Rita says. "Maybe he hits her or something."

"It's not that," Tiki says, rubbing her temples. "But I can't talk any more about it."

"Poor Tiki," says Agnes. "You must have been so worried." And what about Nyssa's grandfather, thinks Agnes. How must he feel?

That next morning Agnes is already awake when reveille plays. As soon as everybody's feet hit the floor, she is fully dressed. She doesn't even bother to do anything to her hair.

"Tiki and Willow?" Agnes says. "Can I have permission to visit Nyssa at Finney's quarters?"

"You could try, Agnes," says Tiki. "But it's up to Finney."

"Maybe it'll help to tell Finney you have something to deliver." Willow produces a paper bag from her duffel. Agnes recognizes the stick-on bow.

"Poor old guy," Tiki says with a sad smile.

Agnes carries the bag, careful not to make it more wrinkly and sad-looking than it already is.

Entering Finney's office, Agnes has no idea what to expect from a Nyssa who would run away.

"Mrs. Finney?" says Agnes. "Hello?"

She tries knocking on the door to Finney's private quarters. Slowly, Agnes turns the doorknob and pokes her head in.

Nyssa is there on her knees, busy refolding the clothes in her duffel bag. "Finney's not here. And I'm not going to say any good-byes," she says.

"Not even to me?"

Nyssa looks Agnes in the eyes. "Nope."

"Then I won't say good-bye either," says Agnes. "But what I do want to know is why you hurt your grandfather like that? Rita thinks he must have hit you to make you act this way."

"He doesn't hit me," says Nyssa quietly.

"I'm wondering something else, then," Agnes says, crossing her arms. "It can't be just because he embarrasses you, can it?"

"My grandfather and me," Nyssa says, "have nothing in common except my mother. Who I barely remember."

"But he's your family," Agnes says.

"My grandfather is the *anti-me*. He doesn't have one honest bone in his body," Nyssa says. "All he wants to do is pretend to like people so he can sell them things! I can't stand it."

"But he cares about you, Nyssa. I can tell."

"No, he doesn't. I'm not supposed to have any private thoughts. He says I spend too much time in my room writing. Before I left, he even took away my notebooks." She bangs her fist once over her heart. "My *notebooks!*"

"Well, that must have been awful," Agnes says. "I'm sorry."

"That's not all. He hates my best friend—always telling me she's bad news. He thinks he knows more about her than *I* do."

"So, he jumps to conclusions," says Agnes. "If *I'm* going to be honest, I'd have to say that sounds sort of familiar."

Nyssa's forehead seems as if she doesn't understand for a moment. Then she sits up and hastily adjusts her glasses. "It doesn't matter anymore," she says. "One year ago, I made a decision. I changed my name. I decided to make myself into the kind of person that *I* want to be, whatever the stupid pressure people put on me. Including him. Or *you*."

"Me?" Agnes lets this remark sink in. "Oh," she says.

"*Oh,*" Nyssa echoes.

Agnes stands there awkwardly until she remembers the paper bag Mr. Vanderhoven left for Nyssa. "He brought you a present."

Nyssa takes the bag. She almost throws it in her duffel. But then she weighs it in her hand, reconsiders, opens the top, and takes out a pen. It's black with a shiny silver nib. Nyssa stares at it and her expression softens. With a look of mystification, she takes out another pen and another. Finally she pulls out a bottle of violet-colored ink and holds it up to the light.

"Calligraphy pens," says Agnes.

Nyssa drops the pens in her lap and hangs her head. "It's not like him," she says. "I don't get it."

"What do you mean?"

"I can't talk now, Agnes."

"Nyssa, I think he's saying he's sorry."

"Please go," she says.

Agnes waits. "I will miss you, Nyssa Noreen Vanderhoven, whoever you are," she says, backing out the door. "I really will."

As Agnes leaves, she almost collides with Mrs. Finney and her cup of morning coffee.

"Excuse me for going in there," says Agnes. "I had to drop off something for Nyssa."

"Did you have a chance to talk to her?" Finney asks.

"She's mad. You know, upset."

"Yes, I know," Finney says. "I tried to get her to stay, Agnes. I want you to know that."

"Really?" says Agnes. "You mean, it was her decision to go?"

"She's very hard to reach, I'm afraid," Finney says.

"Well," says Agnes, "can I ask you to maybe try again? The thing her grandfather sent her? I really think it had an effect."

"I'll try," said Finney.

Agnes walks to the edge of the lake to think. She picks up a pebble, throws it, listens to the plop, and watches the circles grow apart on top of the water. When the water grows still again, she throws another.

I am losing friends, she thinks. And I'm not used to that.

Agnes knows that if her own grandfather had sent her those pens, any anger she felt would have dissolved. Is that because she has *less* integrity?

Agnes throws another rock and . . . stops. A smile spreads over her face. She turns her back on the lake and walks toward Finney's office.

The door is open. Finney is at her desk with pen and paper.

"I'm back already," Agnes says. "Any luck?"

"Afraid not," says Mrs. Finney. "Her grandfather is due to pick her up this evening after work."

"Can I see her? One more time?"

Finney gestures toward the back room. "Take your shot."

Nyssa, who is lying on her stomach, writing in her notebook, seems surprised to see Agnes.

"I'm going to give you another chance," says Agnes.

"What?"

"I'm going to give you another chance to admit that *you're* the chicken!"

"I am not," says Nyssa, "a chicken. And why are you smiling at me like that?"

"Because I realized that you are just scared. That's all. You tell me I'm wimpy for being loyal and caring for other people's feelings, but YOU never give anybody second chances because you're scared. Not fair—*scared.*"

"Thanks for the psychology. But no thanks," says Nyssa.

"So, are you still going home?" asks Agnes.

"Yes."

"Then I'll give you a THIRD chance."

"You are acting completely weird, you know," Nyssa says.

"I don't care," says Agnes. She sits on the floor next to Nyssa's bed. "Why would you go home to your grandfather if he's the one you're mad at?"

"Because I don't want to explain myself to anyone here."

"Because you're *afraid.* You freaked out. And now

everyone in the cabin knows what makes you feel bad. And you are embarrassed about that."

Nyssa picks up her pen and starts doodling again. "I suppose you'd stay, right?"

"Yes, I would. I'm used to being a chicken. Plus, I'm used to giving people lots of chances. For me, it's just not a big weakness." Agnes rests her chin on Nyssa's mattress. "I just decided this, you know."

Nyssa turns on her side and props up on an elbow. "Well, it seems to me you've pretty much written off your old best friend. Are you planning to give her some more of your famous chances too?"

"Is this a challenge?" Agnes asks.

Nyssa sits up. Her gray eyes almost sparkle. "I'll tell you what, Agnes Parker. I'll stay . . ."

"Woo-hoo!" squeals Agnes.

Nyssa holds up a hand. "Wait. I was going to say, I'll stay—if you walk your talk."

"Aye," Agnes says. "A catch."

Nyssa shows a hint of a smile. "I dare you, Agnes Parker, to sit at the Fawns' table at lunch, right next to Prejean Duval. Totally uninvited. AND you have to stay until you've cleaned your entire tray."

"You want me to sit next to her and *eat*?"

"Not just eat. You have to give her one of your second chances. It's a two-in-one test."

"How's that?" Agnes asks.

"Because you have to be brave and swallow your pride at the same time," says Nyssa. "And if you can do that, not only will I stay; you will be my hero forever."

"And . . . do I get to call you Noreen?"

"No," says Nyssa firmly.

"Okay," says Agnes. "Deal."

Agnes is beamingly happy as Nyssa tells Finney she's going to stay. And that's nothing compared to the sense of triumph she feels as she leads Nyssa back to the Mallard cabin.

"Prepare to be love-bombed!" says Agnes, shoving open the door.

"Are you staying?" asks Tiki.

"Oh, Nyssa!" says Willow.

Agnes loves seeing how Nyssa forgets to make her scowly face as that quacking gang of girls rush to welcome her back.

"See?" says Agnes. "You're a perfect Mallard!"

"And so are you, Agnes Parker," says George, pulling her into the group hug.

"Cluck!" says Nyssa.

"Cluck?" asks Beth.

"Haven't you heard?" says Nyssa. "It seems I have a bit of chicken in me."

Agnes just smiles.

CHAPTER 12

AGNES'S JOB THIS MORNING IS to help Willow mix up the plaster of paris that the Mallards will use to make casts of animal tracks. She stirs absently as the other campers tease her bunk buddy.

"Could have used this stuff to track Nyssa yesterday," says George.

"It would have been easy too," says Rita, "with those clompers she wears."

"Am I going to be the butt of all the jokes today?" Nyssa asks.

"Definitely," laughs SPF.

Agnes listens but doesn't join in. Instead, she pictures the cold shoulder—or worse—she's sure to receive at lunch from the horrible Fawns. Will they boo me? Throw food? How else would she expect them to treat the girl who got caught filling their bathing suit bottoms with chocolate?

"Hey, Agnes," says Lisette softly. "You okay?"

"Oh, yeah," she says. "Fine." But can Nyssa really hold her to something she promised in a moment of overenthusiasm?

"While you guys are mixing, why don't some of us go out and look for tracks?" suggests SPF.

"Yeah," says George. "Seems like a better idea than carrying plaster all over the forest while we hunt for them."

"I'll go," says Nyssa, "if you guys promise to stop making fun of me."

"Uh, no," says George. "But why don't you come anyway?"

Willow sets out individual cans for each Mallard in the dusty earth surrounding the cabin. Agnes follows close behind, trying to half-fill each can without making a mess. Is nervousness making me shaky? she wonders, as she glops the white stuff down the side of her shoes.

"Hey," says Willow. "You want me to do that?"

"Maybe you should," says Agnes.

Willow takes the big can from Agnes's hands. "That was a good thing you did, Agnes," she says.

"Thanks," says Agnes, wiping plaster drips from her shoes.

After the cans are neatly filled, Agnes and Willow lean against the cabin waiting for the trackers to return. "So, Agnes, what *did* you do to get Nyssa to stay? If you don't mind my askin'."

"I sold my soul, that's all," Agnes says.

"Hmm," Willow says. "Wonder why Finney never thought of that."

"Because she's smarter than I am," Agnes says without hesitation.

"You guys!" Kacy shrieks. "George is back. She found tracks!"

"We think they're tracks," says SPF. "They're these skinny holes in the mud by the lake."

"Probably deer," says Willow.

Nyssa steps up to Agnes. "I found something else," she says. "Over by the bathroom. Want to check it out?"

"Sure," Agnes says halfheartedly. "What do you think you've got?"

"A five-hundred-pound gorilla," Nyssa says.

Agnes pauses. "You've got your sarcasm back, I see," she says, picking up her can of plaster.

"Just follow me," Nyssa says.

When the two girls round the corner at the cement lavatory, Agnes stops short. Standing there is none other than Natalie Kim.

Natalie springs back and holds her hands up. "What have you got in that can?"

"Plaster," says Agnes, flummoxed.

"Don't worry, Natalie," Nyssa says. "This isn't a trap or anything."

Natalie narrows her eyes.

"The plaster is for animal tracks," says Nyssa.

"Oh," Natalie says, relaxing. "You just never know. What with this whole rivalry thing. Which is incredibly stupid, by the way."

"I agree," Agnes says. She notes that Natalie avoids speaking directly to her. So why is she hanging around?

"Agnes," Nyssa begins, "I've been doing a little investigating . . ."

"Snooping, actually," Natalie says. "And she wants me to tell you the whole Prejean story."

"There's a whole story?" says Agnes.

"The first thing is, you know you and Prejean are best friends," says Natalie, warming. "Are you as stubborn as she is?"

"Actually, I don't think anyone is."

"You're probably right," says Natalie. "And here's your perfect example: that night at campfire already with that spin the bottle game? Prejean went because everybody dared her that she wouldn't."

"That sounds typical," says Agnes. "She's always been like that."

"So we get there, right? And Prejean spins, and she gets this little guy."

"Yeah, I heard about this," says Agnes. "He got shy and decided he didn't want to play."

Natalie shakes her head. "Who told you that?"

"This guy from the Moose cabin," Agnes says. "He says he saw the whole thing."

"Agnes," says Nyssa, "Natalie says the kid didn't want to kiss Prejean because she's *black*."

Agnes puts her hand to her mouth. "What?" Agnes says. "You're kidding!"

"No. He even said something like, 'My parents would kill me if they found out I kissed a black,'" says Natalie.

"Those were his words," says Nyssa. "A *black*. Tell her what Prejean did next."

Agnes listens to how Prejean stepped up to the kid and grabbed him by the front of the shirt. How she pulled him up from the ground . . .

"His eyes were like, bulging!" says Natalie.

"From total fear," adds Nyssa.

"And she gave him this full-on monster kiss!" says Natalie. "I thought he was going to die."

"Then," says Nyssa, "she set the boy back down and said . . ."

"DEAL WITH IT," finishes Natalie. "It was . . . *very* cool."

Put this way, Agnes can now picture the entire scene. It is the exact thing Prejean would do—even before she grew those six inches. Agnes laughs out loud. "I should have known!" she says.

"Prejean doesn't 'do' scared," Natalie says. "It's her weakness."

"What a funny thing to say," says Agnes. "But true. You know, Nyssa, Prejean reminds me a little bit of you."

"Yes, precisely," Nyssa says. "Except . . ." She appears to be searching for the words. "I have another point."

"Yes?" says Agnes.

"If I'm going to be honest, I realize I said things that were unfair. About Prejean. *Obviously,* she's black. Am I the blackness monitor? No. So, seeing that this has been on my conscience, I issue a very sincere apology."

"Good," says Agnes.

"Another thing," says Natalie. "Prejean won't tell you this, but not having you to talk to has been real hard on her. Actually, after that kiss she looked like she might want to cry. But she just went off by herself."

"Oh, Nat," Agnes says. "Really?"

"I will leave you two," says Nyssa, folding her hands, "as I believe my work here is done."

"Uh, thanks," says Agnes. But mine, she thinks, is not.

The picnic tables are already crowded when Agnes gets up the courage to go to lunch. On her tray she has only an orange. She doesn't know if she can manage anything more. The Fawns are over at a corner table with a counselor at either end. The closer she gets, the blurrier everyone looks. She can almost hear her own heartbeat th-thumping in her ears.

Agnes catches Natalie's eye. Natalie, who is sitting facing Prejean, purses her lips to suppress a smile. Agnes can see the back of Prejean's "Fawn" ponytail, her sharp shoulder blades, and lanky arms. When she's finally inches behind her, holding her tray, the rest of the Fawns look up and fall silent.

Prejean turns around. "Agnes?" she says.

"Hi," Agnes says. "Can I sit here?"

Prejean, looking stunned, just opens her mouth.

"Please?" Agnes asks.

"*You* want to sit *here?*" It's an eighth-grade girl with bulging blue eyes. "With the FAWNS?"

"I'm, uh, yes . . ." she stammers.

"What's up with that?" says another girl. "I don't get it. Aren't you that Mallard girl?"

"Actually," Agnes rasps, "I just wanted . . . I was trying . . ." She swallows hard, trying to unstick her words.

Prejean stands up. "This," she says commandingly, "is Agnes Parker. And she is my *best friend.*"

The Fawns all sit quietly.

"Since second grade," says Agnes.

"Here," says Prejean, patting the bench. "By me."

Agnes exhales, and then she sits. She and Prejean look at each other for a long time—until the edges of Prejean's mouth start to twitch. With a sputter, she breaks into her familiar, snorty, wide-mouth laugh. Before Agnes knows it, she is laughing too.

"It's you!" says Agnes, giving Prejean a shove. "The same old you. I can't believe I was scared for even a second."

"Did you really really hate my guts?" Prejean asks.

"Not hate!" says Agnes. "Maybe I was a little jealous of 'your guts.' And Natalie's."

"How in the world did you get the nerve to come over here?"

"Oh, Prejean," says Agnes, "don't you know I always give in first?"

"I think it's because she's sensible," says Natalie.

"And also because," says Prejean, her eyes moistening, "you're terminally nice." She sighs and squeezes Agnes's arm. "I missed you so much."

"Me too," says Agnes, tearing up. "Not because you're terminally nice, though, of course."

Prejean laughs. "Then why?"

"Because you're my . . . Prejean!" Agnes says. "And I don't know where to get another one."

Every day for the last week of camp, Agnes eats at both her table and with Prejean at lunch. Most of the

Fawns don't seem to mind anymore. And when she bumps into Prejean and Nat at the lodge or at the lake, they wave and smile. But most of the time, Agnes hangs out with her Mallards.

"You're back," Nyssa says, always a little surprised, when Agnes catches up with her in the afternoon.

"Back with a quack," says George. "Just like me and SPF."

"Once a Mallard, always a Mallard," says SPF.

It's true, thinks Agnes. Four weeks ago, she never would have guessed.

At the last campfire, the girls in her cabin sit up long into the night. The black sky is saturated with stars.

"I don't want to go to sleep tonight," says Beth. "Because when we wake up, camp will be really over."

"You're going to make me cry, Beth," says Lisette.

"Wait 'til tomorrow," says Rita. "Everybody cries."

"Even the tough girls," says George.

Night seems to pass in a blink, and the trumpet sputters the strains of the last reveille as the hot morning light streams through the windows.

"Rise and shine, Mallards!" says Willow.

"Up and at 'em," says Tiki. "Time to pack it up."

"Awwwww," says SPF. "Can't we have just a few more minutes?"

Beth and Lisette sit up together. "It's the last day!" says Lisette.

"I'm going to miss you guys . . . so much!" says Beth.
They simultaneously burst into tears.

"Oh, no," says George. "Not already. It's way too early." And then she breaks down.

Tiki and Willow go around dispensing tissues and embraces. "You are the best group of girls I've ever had," Tiki says, sniffling.

Agnes glances at Nyssa, who seems numbed by the scene.

"I can't do this," Nyssa says, getting up.

"Where are you going?" cries Kacy.

"Just outside," says Agnes, following Nyssa. "For a sec."

"Remember," says Nyssa as soon as she and Agnes are safely outside, "what I told you the first day? When I said I can't be a happy camper?"

"Of course," says Agnes. "It's burned in my memory."

"Well, I can't be a crying camper either," she says.

Agnes puts her arm around Nyssa's shoulders. "And I can't believe I'm *not* crying," she says. "What has this place done to us?"

"Don't know," says Nyssa. "Let's just take a walk."

The girls make their way barefoot into the nearby clearing. A flock of small birds flutter up from the grass. The sun shines on, in its insistent summer way. They plop down, drenching the seats of their pj's in dew and, for a while, sit in comfortable silence.

Nyssa smiles. "Thank you, Agnes," she says.

"For what?" Agnes says.

"This. It's perfect. Most people would have messed it up." Nyssa give a satisfied sigh. "I'm glad I picked you," she says.

"But you didn't," Agnes says. "The camp chose for us."

"No, I mean afterward. When it was totally up to me. I PICKED YOU." Nyssa stands and offers Agnes a hand up. "Enough said."

The two stand for a moment more until Agnes hears singing in the distance. "It's that campfire song," she says. "Take me there, I wanna go there." She hums, picking up the melody.

The singing gets closer, louder. It's the Mallards, led by George, who walk-dances, holding her flashlight like a microphone.

"We made a deal," SPF shouts. "We decided to cry on the way home!"

"I think," murmurs Agnes to Nyssa, "that this is their present to you."

"Cool," says Nyssa, genuinely pleased.

George sings it again, this time wiggling her behind and throwing up one hand like a diva. The other Mallards clap.

Take me there, I wanna go there,
Take me there! I've been nowhere!

Take me to that great place of wonders and wishes.
Take me there, I wanna go there,
Take me there! Let's go there!
Blue lake and campfires, and moonlight and fishes!

Take me there, I wanna go there, they chant. They move in a circle, every girl dancing in her own way. Beth and Lisette hop forward like bunnies. Kacy twirls. Rita walks bent-kneed and low to the ground. Tiki clicks her fingers like a flamenco dancer. Willow slouches, heel-toeing like a cowgirl. George strums an imaginary electric guitar. SPF does the hula. Nyssa bobs her head very slightly, and Agnes makes like a swimmer going down.

These are my . . . my four-week friends! And maybe more.

Agnes takes it in, sight and sound, like a movie camera. She knows that whatever the new year brings, whenever she hums "Take Me There," she'll be thinking of this summer, these girls, this moment.

KATHLeeN O'DeLL
EXPERIENCED CAMPER

IN SIXTH GRADE KATHLEEN O'DELL went to Outdoor School—a camp dedicated to teaching kids about nature and ecology. At this camp there really was a dirt-expert named Sandy who ate soil. There was also a fashion show where the campers wore the odds and ends of one another's suitcases. Kathy shot her first bow and arrow there and made the surprising discovery that she was a better shot without her glasses. With them, she frequently missed the target altogether.

Kathy remembers being very aware of the boys at the camp. She and most of her friends tried hard to pretend that they didn't care about or notice them. But secretly, she checked for signs that she might be considered "girlfriend material." With middle school looming, she began to wonder which of the girls she knew would be sought after and socially successful, and which would be left behind in dorkdom. Adding to her anxiety, Kathy's mom had written her name in permanent market in all her underwear, including her brand-new bras. This produced nightmares that a bra would somehow fall out of her suitcase and there'd be an announcement over the camp loudspeaker saying: KATHLEEN O'DELL, PLEASE PICK UP YOUR BRAND-NEW BRA AT THE FRONT OFFICE! Kathy hid her bras in the lining of her suitcase and checked every day to make sure they were still there. Though she didn't want to be overlooked entirely, she wasn't anywhere near ready for that much attention from the boys (or anyone else).

In spite of this initial awkwardness, Kathy ended up having such a great time at camp that she cried when she had to leave. Some of her friends even went on to become camp counselors. Today Kathy satisfies her camp nostalgia by watching repeated showings of the movie *The Parent Trap*. She hopes readers will have as much fun in the pages of this story as she did in her own happy camping days.